A N I M A L S

ANIMALS

T. TROUGHTON

A Touchstone Book
LONDON . SYDNEY . NEW YORK . TOKYO
SINGAPORE . TORONTO

First published in Great Britain by Touchstone, 1998
A division of Simon & Schuster Ltd
A Viacom Company

Simon & Schuster Ltd
West Garden Place
Kendal Street
London
W2 2AQ

SIMON & SCHUSTER AUSTRALIA
SYDNEY

A CIP catalogue record for this book is available
from the British Library.

ISBN 0−684−81946 5

1 3 5 7 9 10 8 6 4 2

Typeset in Melior by Palimpsest Book Production Limited,
Polmont, Stirlingshire
Printed and bound in Great Britain by
Cox & Wyman Ltd., Reading, Berkshire

Thanks to Geoff, Gillon, Emma,
Al and M & P.

O N E

It is around three in the afternoon, which is not a bad time on the whole, and I have got up & shaved & brushed my teeth and found my way to our usual caff, where I am testing out whatever is in my cup and thinking about nothing in particular. It being Saturday the place is packed with exhausted & miserable shoppers, who are seeming none too cheered by what Anna the mediterranean manageress calls refreshments, but no one looks like doing much about it, as Anna is six foot tall with a fine moustache and a glint in her eye which suggests they are better off simply swallowing it.

So I am doing the sensible thing, and once I have my refreshment and can get my head round things a little I notice my table is full of the finest examples of local culture, or at any rate those who survive the night. And it is becoming clear they have only one topic of conversation, which is a recent accident to a person known to all & sundry as Mick-ther-man, on the grounds that this is what he calls himself.

And it appears that twelve hours before, Mick-ther-man jumps in a reckless sort of way out of a top-floor window, and everyone round the table is highly upset & concerned as a result. I am surprised, since Mick-ther-man is not a pleasant person and probably never will be; in fact it would not bother me any to hear that his exploits are over permanently instead of just on hold in accident & emergency. But everyone else is wondering who will take over supplying them with dangerous & illegal substances, which is how Mick-ther-man makes his money, and which arrangement keeps everyone happy, apart from their neighbours.

So the whole table is puzzling over this, and some of them are complaining, and quite a few are looking a little edgy already, when someone suggests hopefully that maybe Mick-ther-man will get better.

But the general opinion is maybe not, or at least not quickly enough to take up supplying again at the rate of demand. It is quite a large and varied demand, and as dealers are fairly uncommon in small market towns the chances of finding a replacement, everyone is working out sadly, are slightly less than Aylesbury Wanderers' chances of making the third or even the fourth division, Aylesbury Wanderers being the local footy team.

*   *   *

'And it depends what you mean by him getting better,' adds a waitress who is bending over the table at the time. Since before Mick-ther-man springs into action he is seemingly downing tabs as if they are on special offer, and is now under the impression that his pelvis is not fractured in seventeen places but is merely melting, and is shortly to be replaced by NASA rocket technology, this being the kind of subject Mick-ther-man interests himself in in the first place. 'Though he is,' the waitress continues, 'surprised to find everyone around him is speaking backwards,' after which news a somewhat despondent silence descends over the table until the waitress takes the hint & departs for wherever waitresses go when they are not centre stage bothering people.

And for a time it looks as though no one will ever speak again, but suddenly the general gloom is shattered by voices raised in anger, and someone mutters that they wish Bernie and his sister would give it a rest. And although none of the table are surprised by the argument, several mothers and small infants in the caff look quite shocked, because insulting and personal comments are being exchanged by both sides followed by language which has many of the mothers turning slightly pale, especially when their infants start repeating it.

*   *   *

Now Bernie is a small & minor person who is generally slow to anger, being a forgiving & christian type, though not in the religious sense, but currently he is shouting you what you what and so on in fury, and his frame appears to be quivering with emotion, although knowing Bernie it is possibly just the shakes.

At any rate his loving sister, who could fit Bernie down one leg of her trousers should she be inclined, is not intimidated, but is repeating many slurs on Bernie's character, and also on that of his long-term companion & soulmate, this being an unsavoury type known only to the general community as Clive, which is how everyone is content to leave it.

And Bernie is saying say that again, and his sister obliges, and this goes on for some time until one of the table says they think everyone has got the message, unfounded though it may be.

Bernie's sister replies with conviction that if it is unfounded she is prepared to eat her hat, adding that Bernie is enjoying Clive's company day & night & the twilight hours in addition. And when asked what they think Clive & Bernie are finding to get up to, the table cannot think of a suitable reply, which Bernie's sister appears to feel proves her point.

'It is disgusting,' she says in conclusion. 'Not to

mention against the laws of nature. He will burn in hell.'

This turns out to be her parthian shot, as she gets up and exits the caff leaving Bernie staring sadly at the remains of his cornish pasty. And a person enquires kindly where Clive is, since no one is taking Bernie's sister at all seriously, but at this question Bernie turns a curious shade of light grey and does not reply.

'I think I will be off,' he says eventually. 'Someone can have my pasty if they want.'

So Bernie departs, presumably back to his village to get up to whatever, and it seems this is the signal for everyone else to make a move. I decline various offers to visit the Kings Head or the Bell or the civic centre, as it looks as though the caff is about to experience a brief and unusual period of calm. Besides, Anna is nodding & winking at me in the way which usually means she would like a word, and indeed as soon as everyone leaves she advances on the table like a black widow spider on a fly, if not faster.

And it seems that Anna hears all about Mick-ther-man's nosedive, and consequently has a business proposal that she claims will benefit the whole community and which any enterprising young person would jump at. As it happens the proposal does sound attractive, but there follows a period of bargaining which Anna naturally gets the better of, seeing as how they are old hands at it in her part of the world. So once we agree on her terms and both of us are happy, Anna returns to lurk behind her counter and I wander out of the caff and in the general direction of the Kings Head, as I am feeling like a bevvy or two to mark the occasion.

Outside there is the usual assortment of prams, shopping trolleys, little old ladies, beer cans, etc, and in the middle of it all is a disconsolate newsvendor trying to force copies of the Bucks Free Press on to anything passing, and not having much joy because, as its name suggests, the Bucks Free Press is the kind of local paper they are lucky to give away. This week its front page consists of an imposing picture of a strangled goose on what looks to be a mortuary slab and, although you cannot tell the goose is strangled from its photo, there is not much doubt that it is dead. Its eyes are shut and its neck is limp, and all in all it looks fairly oven ready and, if you are partial to goose, probably quite appetising, even if this is not the photographer's original intention.

And the newsvendor is shouting, 'Latest in Chiltern Goose Strangler horror' in a dramatic way, but no one wants to know, since they are all having it up to here with the Chiltern Goose Strangler, who is occupying the front page of the Bucks Free Press for weeks, and who is so far showing no sign of strangling anything more interesting e.g. children, but is sticking to what is generally felt to be a limited repertoire.

But I am almost duty bound to pick up a copy, because the Chiltern Goose Strangler is none other than my uncle Nigel, or to be precise, my ex-uncle Nigel, ever since my aunt takes the rest of the family's advice and gets shot of him. And although ex-uncle Nigel naturally keeps his alter ego a closely guarded secret, I happen to meet him late one night carrying two dead geese under one arm and humming to himself, and generally looking like a man with a favourite hobby, if a somewhat peculiar one. At the time even ex-uncle Nigel admits it looks suspicious, and gives me an ingratiating smile saying honestly son, I can explain everything. But after a pause he says he has never much fancied geese anyway, and would bet a week's dole that, if he could remember any of his childhood, he would recall being viciously assaulted by a flock during a day-trip to a farm or something similar. Then he adds that there is a regular goose explosion in these parts, and many of them are banged up in dark barns and so on, so really it is a kindness to put them out of their misery.

Sadly, the police are not seeing his activities in this light. Indeed after the fiftieth goose or so they are running around like headless chickens, but despite their best efforts no one seems able to stop what the Bucks Free Press regularly refers to as this twisted maniac. And ex-uncle Nigel confides that he has often enjoyed a quiet chuckle over their confusion, and actually seems to be getting quite a kick out of being dubbed the Chiltern Goose Strangler, as previously his only nickname is Nobby.

Ever since our encounter ex-uncle Nigel's career is going from strength to strength, so I am surprised to find that, according to today's Bucks Free Press, a man has just been arrested in connection with the deaths of ninety-seven local geese. Although the paper does not give his name, there is a little photo of a blanket at the bottom of the page, which apparently is the person in question getting into a police van. And the Bucks Free Press special reporter explains that there are fears for his safety following threats from infuriated goose owners, because it seems the Chiltern Goose Strangler did not stop at strangling, as indeed the paper hints by means of a headline saying IS IT THE CHILTERN GOOSE MOLESTER TOO? And many goose owners who found their geese cold & lifeless in the morning have not given them a decent burial but eaten them instead, and are apparently now feeling more than a little sick about it.

I am thinking how it takes all sorts and so on, when suddenly I feel a hand on my shoulder and turn round to see a balding little bloke with beady little eyes and a general air of having a gerbil in his not-so-distant ancestry. And it is ex-uncle Nigel, without a blanket or policeman in sight.

He is saying it is all a mistake and he has not been arrested, someone else has, which is obvious, as ex-uncle Nigel would have trouble breaking out of a playpen never mind a police cell. And after we find a quiet park bench and ex-uncle Nigel has had many restorative nips from a scotch bottle, he says he is relying on me for advice as I remind him of himself when he was my age, and although he obviously thinks this is flattering, it is not.

On close inspection ex-uncle Nigel looks even worse than usual, as he is covered with cuts and bruises and has a melancholy & desperate look on his face, on top of which he appears to have been rolling in goose dung. His voice is trembling with outrage, especially when he informs me that he never lays so much as a finger on a goose except to strangle it, and that the Chiltern Goose Molester headline is making him seriously consider suing the Bucks Free Press for defamation of character.

It turns out that last night ex-uncle Nigel is out quietly strangling as usual, and has a productive & satisfying session, and says everything would be fine if he just goes straight home as he usually does afterwards. But he does not, because he sees a deserted old farmhouse en route, and goes to check it is properly locked & secured, since people can never be too careful these days. But he rapidly regrets his action. Because lurking behind the farmhouse is yet another goose, and ex-uncle Nigel has had enough of geese for one evening and by now only feels up to wrapping his hands around his bedtime bovril.

So he is preparing to leave sharpish when the goose sees him and takes an instant aversion to him, and before you know it there is an almighty punch-up and feathers fly and, after being pecked quite nastily, ex-uncle Nigel wins. Which the goose if it had stopped to think about things might have predicted, as although ex-uncle Nigel is not an olympic specimen by any stretch of the imagination he is still quite considerably larger than most geese and knows a lot more about tactics etc.

Unfortunately by this stage it is obvious that the farmhouse is not deserted at all, as there are lights flashing on all over the place and shouts of get my gun, and to his horror ex-uncle Nigel hears the thunder of footsteps on the stairs, closely followed by the bang of a door opening with more than the usual force.

But when whoever it is skids to a halt in the yard

they find it is empty, since ex-uncle Nigel is cowering under a heap of goose dung in what turns out to be the farm's main goose barn, and praying that his cunning, if somewhat ironic, hiding place will not be discovered. It is not, although the search goes on for hours, and about half-way through ex-uncle Nigel finds to his surprise that goose dung is quite warm and comfortable, especially for someone who is up & physically active all night.

Some time later he is woken by the sound of rustling and muted squawking, and reckoning that the search must be over by now he pokes his head out cautiously. In the wavering light of a torchbeam he sees, to his astonishment, a huge black-clad figure clutching a goose in one hand and what looks to be a roll of masking tape in the other. Ex-uncle Nigel has no idea what the figure can be up to, but it is obviously nothing good as the figure is wearing a kind of Zorro mask and is chuckling evilly to itself.

As ex-uncle Nigel watches, the figure examines the goose it is holding and says, 'A female', in disgusted tones and chucks the goose away, and the goose looks as surprised as ex-uncle Nigel and, unusually for a goose, remains just as quiet, since its beak has been taped up with a practised hand.

The figure picks up another goose, and much the same

thing happens, and there is getting to be quite a pile of rejected geese by the time the figure finds one that takes its fancy. Ex-uncle Nigel says that what happens next turns his stomach, and the goose does not seem to be enjoying it much either, although the figure is apparently having the time of its life and is shouting way hey and take it big boy and other such endearments.

But once the figure finishes it does not appear to be grateful. Instead it despatches the goose with a kind of crunching noise, which ex-uncle Nigel should be used to by now, but which oddly makes him twitch a little with discomfort. And the figure must see the twitch out of the corner of an eye, because it says, 'Who is that?' in startled tones, and ex-uncle Nigel loses his nerve completely and tries to make a run for it.

This turns out to be a mistake, as the figure is after him like a ferret down a bolthole, and no matter how much ex-uncle Nigel dodges and weaves and throws geese into its path, the result is that he is shortly lying on the ground, trussed and bound with baling twine, and his mouth is being taped up too and the figure is saying, 'One more goose and then it's your go, matey.'

Ex-uncle Nigel has never felt much of an affinity with geese, quite the reverse, but as he sees the figure go through its preparations he begins to experience something like empathy with the goose in question, and once the figure gets into its stride, ex-uncle Nigel closes his eyes and swears that if he gets out of this one he will never so much as eat a goose again, not even in pâté.

Eventually there are the sounds of things coming to a climax, followed by another sad little crunch, and ex-uncle Nigel unscrews his eyes a fraction to be greeted by a full frontal of the figure advancing towards him with a predatory smile on its lips. And for a second, ex-uncle Nigel says, he is reminded of my aunt, though this homely thought does not make him feel any better. He begins to struggle against his bonds while grunting desperately through the masking tape, but the twine just gets tighter and the figure closer, and the latter is saying approvingly, 'That's right, I like something with a bit of fight in it,' at which ex-uncle Nigel immediately goes limp and still and makes little whining noises. But this ploy merely causes the figure to rub its hands together and remark that, then again, passive is good too, so it looks like ex-uncle Nigel is stuffed either way.

The figure then rolls ex-uncle Nigel over so he is face down on the ground, and disappears behind him. Of course, now ex-uncle Nigel cannot see a thing, for which he is quite grateful. All he can do is grit his teeth & think of England, and it is only after he goes through all the home counties and is thinking nostalgically of Aberystwyth, where he once went on a coach trip, that it occurs to him he has been waiting rather a long time.

So he stops thinking and listens, and from behind him he hears pacing and cursing and the sound of a frustrated groan or two. Then the figure appears to make up its mind, because a pair of size-twelve black plimsolls appears in front of ex-uncle Nigel's nose and a voice from above says in somewhat embarrassed tones, 'Sorry, it's just not working.'

Ex-uncle Nigel would say there is no need to apologise on his account, but cannot because of the masking tape, so he grunts instead. And the figure explains that this has never happened before, and adds that the problem seems to be that it just does not find ex-uncle Nigel attractive.

Ex-uncle Nigel feels rather wounded by this, but also relieved, and there is a pause while the figure hums and hars, and then it says, 'I'm taking off the tape but don't make a sound, I've got a knife,' and rips off the masking tape, after which there is another pause while ex-uncle Nigel tries to scream with agony very very quietly, being under the impression that half of his face has come off with it.

*   *   *

The figure considerately waits for him to finish, and once he has done so it squats down in front of him and says, 'Cackle.'

When ex-uncle Nigel whispers what? in surprise, the figure says you know, like a goose, and waves its knife in front of his eyes in an encouraging manner.

At this moment ex-uncle Nigel realises he is dealing with someone who is several sarnies short of a picnic, in fact under the circumstances he might have realised this sooner, so in desperation he does the only thing he can think of, which is to thrust his head forwards and bite the figure's nose as hard as his false teeth will let him.

There is a huge howl of pain and dismay, and suddenly ex-uncle Nigel feels as though his teeth have been ripped from his mouth by a mighty hand, and from his limited viewpoint he sees a pair of feet staggering backwards and forwards to the accompaniment of shrieks of pain. Finally the feet stagger out of his line of vision and ex-uncle Nigel hears a muffled fuck followed by a resounding crash, and then silence.

Reckoning that he now has nothing to lose, ex-uncle Nigel wriggles energetically until he is the right way up again, and observes a black lump lying on the ground about ten feet away from him. From its position it looks very much as though it has tripped over something and hit its head against an old plough-share, and on looking more closely, ex-uncle Nigel sees that the something it has tripped over is a dead goose.

Later, ex-uncle Nigel will think hoist by his own canard and feel very witty & clever, but not at this moment because all he can think of is retrieving his teeth and getting out of there a.s.a.p. Luckily the figure's knife is close by, and so it is the work of an instant or two to saw through the baling twine, rinse the teeth in an old rain tank and scarper.

As ex-uncle Nigel high-tails it down the drive, he notices that lights are coming on in the farmhouse again, and thinks with some satisfaction that the figure's goose is cooked, as it were, and judging by the revelations in the Bucks Free Press he is right. So when he finishes his story and looks at me expectantly, I say I cannot see what the problem is, as it seems that he has been more than a little lucky, if anything.

But ex-uncle Nigel continues to look distressed. It turns out that he has been boasting to his friends over a few bevvies about being the Chiltern Goose Strangler, and now that the Chiltern Goose Strangler has become inextricably linked with the Chiltern Goose Molester he feels he will never live it down. He says he is sick to death of geese, on top of which he now feels honour bound never to touch one again, and so has already decided there is only one way round it all.

'I am leaving today,' he says. 'For Manchester, where there are no geese to speak of and where hopefully I will get a job & make a fresh start,' and asks if I can lend him a tenner to keep him going in the mean time. I cough up the tenner and wish ex-uncle Nigel all the best and so on, and privately reckon that even in Manchester he will be back on geese within a week, because once this sort of thing is in your blood you are practically doomed to repeat it.

But not long afterwards I get a grubby postcard with pre-war scenes of industrial life in Manchester on the front, and on the back a message saying that ex-uncle Nigel has got a job, exclamation mark. It is, the postcard says proudly, a responsible position on a green poultry farm in Cheshire. Apparently lots of ageing hippies and similar types have started up these enterprises, using only traditional farming methods, because they are kinder than modern methods, or so people believe, and as a result the ageing hippies can charge a fortune per chicken and make another one themselves, which shows pretty good business sense for a hippy.

And ex-uncle Nigel's job title is Deputy Manager – Despatch, which means he is a chicken strangler. As the postcard says, it is right up his alley, and although there are a few sticky moments at the job interview when he is asked about previous work experience etc, at the end of the day he thinks he swung it on the practical.

T W O

So Mick-ther-man is out of hospital and being wheeled round town by his mother. Neither of them looks to be enjoying it much, but at least Mick-ther-man sees melting lampposts and giant sparrows and other interesting visions en route which his mother does not, though she gets to hear all about them. And Mick-ther-man's reappearance is not greeted with much joy by the rest of the community either, since most of them still owe him money and are fearful he will regain his senses long enough to remember who and how much and so on, but after thirteen tabs at once I am not betting on it.

Sadly it turns out that people are fickle even about their dealers, and once they find another source of supply it is as if the first one never existed, especially when his stock is not up to much anyway. The stock I am now getting from Anna the mediterranean manageress's brother, who frequently offloads his fishing vessel at a convenient British port, and whose sister is generally there to welcome him, is top class, or so I am told, and therefore Mick-ther-man is widely agreed to be not only insane but redundant.

But being a dealer is not all it is cracked up to be. Indeed, I am developing a new and increasing respect for Mick-ther-man, because my phone is soon sounding like a car alarm and friends & acquaintances and all & sundry begin dropping round on the off-chance at all hours, and particularly the unsociable ones. It is not as if I am left with much profit after Anna creams off her percentage; nor do I seem to collect the cash from my customers with Mick-ther-man's degree of success, possibly because, unlike Mick-ther-man, I do not possess an extensive collection of knuckledusters. So it is reaching the stage where I am thinking of chucking it in, but am enjoying even the small profit I make too much to get out, which is how people are trapped in this kind of situation, though admittedly they are generally working on production lines & similar.

So I am sitting in a quiet corner of the civic centre one Monday lunchtime with Guy, who is an old friend & acquaintance of mine with whom I often share a few bevvies and so on. And I am dealing with a flood of customers, if not a torrent, and Eddie the civic manager is rubbing his hands together, because of course everyone is buying a coffee or maybe a snack from the bar to make things look regular. There are all sorts of people sidling up to our table, including several little schoolboys who should know better, it being against the rules for them to be off school grounds at lunchtime. They snigger when Guy reminds them of this regulation, but they stop quite quickly after he gives them a look, and I do not blame them, because Guy has a quiet air of menace about him, thanks largely to a variety of tattoos and a down-to-the-wood haircut, and his reputation as leader of the Aylesbury Skins also tends to precede him.

So the schoolboys disappear looking chastened and clutching their wraps in their hot little hands, and will never know that what they think is wicked speed is just talc coloured pink with dyed sugar, because I am against giving gear to the underage in principle, and in any case have to make my profit somewhere. It is looking as though the rush is over, and I am starting to relax and thinking about heading off myself when Guy leans over the table and says he would like a word.

Knowing Guy this probably means that he is falling for a female again, as despite his looks he is the emotional type and inclined to get very wound up about the opposite sex. But instead he tells me that he's recently become involved with the Inter City Firm. I am sorry to hear it, as the ICF are an unpleasant lot who like nothing better than to go to footy matches and kick people's heads in, and do not appreciate the skills of the game at all. But Guy says it is as good a way as any of spending his spare time, and it lets him get about and see the country. Besides, the Aylesbury Skins are running out of heads to kick in, since Aylesbury is a fairly small town and there are only so many times you can kick in the same head without getting bored of the whole business.

But this is beside the point, Guy says. The reason he brings the matter up is that last Saturday he is all set to go and have a blast with the ICF and kick in a few heads and bring home some souvenir scarves from the opposition's necks, when his father turns round & says not bleeding likely, and informs him that his presence is required in the family butcher shop all day. Guy is not unnaturally horrified by this and thinks about kicking his own father's head in, but not for long, as Guy's father is if anything bigger than Guy, although it is a close run thing, and Guy maintains that in a few more years he will have him.

But until that day Guy has no choice but to go along with his father's plans. He puts his supporter's gear back in the cupboard, along with the various weapons he is taking just in case, and drags his feet reluctantly to the shop. Once he is there he finds he is soothed by the routine of cleaning counters and dismembering dead animals and so on, in fact Guy in the butcher's shop is quite a sight, there being no doubt he knows his trade, possibly because of all the practice he puts in with the Aylesbury Skins.

However it turns out that this is a quiet morning for business. Indeed according to Guy's father most mornings these days are quiet, because M & S has just opened up in the town centre and all the people who live in the villages in converted barns with mill wheels now go to M & S for their sausages instead of Green & Son, which is what Guy's father's shop is called. And Guy's father is narked about this no end and is stamping around and saying they are killing us off, we are a dying breed. And Guy is not happy either, because he is thinking that with everything so quiet he could easily have been spared to go and play with the ICF boys, whose business is not quiet at all.

When suddenly there is the ting-ting of the bell above the door and Guy's father's ears prick up like those of an old warhorse who hears a trumpet. Two customers come in, and Guy's ears prick up too because one of the customers is very attractive. In fact, when asked to describe her, Guy turns purple and mutters, but when further encouraged he says she is a class A babe.

But the class A babe does not look equally delighted by the appearance of Green & Son; indeed she looks like she is about to be sick. Guy sees her turn to her friend and say, 'I don't know how you can stand to come in here.' And her friend, who now that Guy is looking appears to be the hippy type, replies, 'I know, I know. Just try not to look. I only have to get Gran her pork loin and it will be over in a second.'

Guy's father throws his eyes up to heaven at this, as pork loin for one old granny is hardly going to keep the family in clover, and retreats to the back of the shop to sulk. Meanwhile Guy is left standing like a statue torn between several emotions, not that statues have emotions. He is, he says, surprised to find that his pride is affronted by this dismissive approach to the family business, and part of him feels like telling them both to take a walk if that is their attitude. But another part of him feels overwhelmingly drawn to the class A babe, and of course this is the part that wins, as it generally does. So he adjusts his apron and steps forward and asks what he can do for her. However the class A babe is keeping her eyes pinned to the ground and does not so much as look at him. It is her friend who speaks instead.

'A small piece of pork loin,' she says. 'And can you hurry? My friend is vegetarian and not used to this kind of thing.' And she turns to the class A babe and asks if she would prefer to wait outside, and the class A babe says no, these things have to be faced sometime, although she still does not look up.

*　　*　　*

Guy is cheered by this reply, and starts tossing the pork loin around with aplomb, but this does not seem to be impressing anyone so he stops and concentrates on spinning it out as long as possible instead. He is keeping a watchful ear on the conversation, and manages to collect that the class A babe has plans for this afternoon, which do not involve the butcher's shop but are more in the line of hunt sabbing. And it seems that the class A babe wishes to know whether her companion is up for it.

At which Guy's heart sinks into his Doc Martens and his hand falters on the meat cleaver, because he is realising that sabbing & vegetarianism are not exactly compatible with his line of trade, but nevertheless, he continues to listen. And the hippy girl is obviously not the kind of person who will put her money where her mouth is, as the saying goes, because while she waxes lyrical about how she would love to come sabbing, and how much she admires the class A babe for doing it every weekend, the upshot is that she is not on for it at all, her excuse being that she has promised to take her mum's peke to the vets.

Guy is not convinced by this and he tells me that the class A babe looks similarly unimpressed, and the two girls leave the shop with friction in the air and the friendship looking as though it is heading for a rocky patch. And never once does the class A babe cast an eye at Guy, although he is trying to intimate by nods and gestures that he supports her. But he says he can tell she is interested and once he puts his plan into action she will fall for him like a ton. I am not persuaded. Despite his many sound qualities, Guy is not exactly strategically minded and the last time he has a plan he omits to check a fairly important fact i.e. whether Radio Rentals put steel shutters on their window at night or not. And it is only when driving a borrowed car at high speed towards the shop that he discovers to his surprise that they do. Luckily no one in the car is damaged, as Guy is quick on the uptake and manages to steer clear at the last minute; but unfortunately he manages to steer towards two Aylesbury Skins who are waiting on the sidelines to help themselves to TVs etc, and there is something of a mess as a result. Indeed for a time it looks as though the Aylesbury Skins who remain will revolt against their leader, but Guy talks firmly to them and they come round to his way of thinking in the end, as they all agree it is safer to have Guy on their side than off it.

So I ask what the plan is this time, but Guy, who may notice a sceptical tone in my voice, looks mysterious and just a little defensive and tells me to wait and see. So confident is he that he bets me a tenner that when I see him next Monday he will have the class A babe in tow and everything will be roses, and I accept, and wonder what I will spend it on, and think it will probably have to be several bevvies for Guy to console him.

So Guy gathers up his cigs, and makes a rude gesture at Eddie as they are old enemies, in fact Eddie is always trying to work up the bottle to bar Guy but cannot, and we depart, although we pause at the exit to talk to Bernie, who is hanging around in a morose way and generally looking like someone who loses his mother. He perks up noticeably when he sees us, and Guy says how are you doing, to which Bernie replies in the same vein, and further pleasantries are swapped in this fashion until Guy asks Bernie where Clive is, at which Bernie suddenly turns green and scuttles off. Though this is not entirely out of character for Bernie, who is frequently acting like a rabbit at the best of times.

Now the following week I hardly have a chance to spare a thought for Guy and the class A babe, since I am not only trying to keep a grip on deliveries, payments etc, which is more than enough work on its own. But one of Mick-ther-man's associates discovers I am newly set up in the business and has started to call me saying he desires a cut, which I cannot afford to give him. And although I explain about profit margins and so on he does not seem to wish to understand, and if anything his phone conversations become more extended and the details even more medical. After which he takes to visiting the places I usually frequent: the civic, the Kings Head, the Bell, the Bull & Bear, the Bugle Horn and so on. While he does not dare to come near Anna's caff, this is little consolation as I do not wish to spend the rest of my life in Anna's caff, or even half of it, so I am forced to take evasive action, with the result that my friends & acquaintances are bemused by my new habit of disappearing in a flash, and the females are of the opinion that I am looking peaky and are trying to feed me vitamins. And the whole situation is highly embarrassing & annoying, but I can see no way of getting round it.

By the end of the week I am a shadow of my former self, and it is only the info that Mick-ther-man's associate is in the habit of going to see his old dad in a rest home of a Monday which gives me any hope of respite. So come Monday I head with relief straight for the civic, where I settle into a quiet corner and concentrate on the first bevvy in ages which it looks like I will have the option to finish.

I am enjoying this brief reprieve when Guy walks in, and with a certain amount of satisfaction I note he does not have a class A babe in tow or anywhere near him. However, I am adjusting my face to the look of sympathy considered necessary under the circumstances, and by the time Guy looms over the table I am commiserating from every pore. So it is irritating to find that I am being slapped on the back and asked if anything is the matter, after which Guy asks breezily what I am having, since the bevvies are on him.

I reply that I am having the usual, and while Guy is humming to himself and pulling out his cigs I enquire what has happened to the class A babe, not that I wish to cast a damper on his mood. Guy gazes around at this and squints & looks generally perplexed, so I remind him that, all things being equal, it looks as though he owes me a tenner. Guy replies that, yes, it would seem he does, but would I mind laying off as he is a little broke at the minute, and continues humming.

Although I have already gathered that Guy's plan does not go according to plan at all, I still wish to know why he is behaving in this cold & heartless fashion, as previously when Guy's romantic endeavours go wrong, as they always do, he is miserable for days and everyone around him suffers, innocent bystanders not excepted. So I repeat my question, to which Guy replies that she is not really a class A babe at all, but more a class D minus one, adding that there are anyway more important things in life than women. At which I look at him suspiciously, and Guy blushes, or begins cracking his knuckles, which for Guy is much the same thing.

And eventually he admits that he is somewhat blinded by the class A babe in the butchers shop that Saturday, so much so that he is not even cheered when his father says they might as well knock off early as it is like a morgue. All Guy can think of is how to get to see the class A babe again, and as he does not know the first or even the second thing about her it seems that all is lost. But then he suddenly realises that he does know one fact, which is that she goes sabbing every weekend. And thanks to her conversation he knows exactly where, so although he has always thought sabbing strictly a game for girls, this now seems to be his only option.

Over many more bevvies he tells me the whole story, which I am not that happy about, as I am loath to give up my afternoon's peace, but once Guy starts talking, or indeed starts anything, it is difficult to stop him, so I am more or less stuck.

Now although the sabbing clashes with both Guy's father's and the ICF's plans for him, such is Guy's infatuation that he does not care. His plan is obviously to go sabbing too, and win the class A babe's affections that way. So he spends all week in anticipation, and does not even cause any bother in case he should get a black eye or a broken nose, or anything similar which might spoil his looks. He also buys a tatty old scarf, and many little badges which say everything from ban the bomb to have a nice day on them, though to my knowledge Guy never subscribes to either of these sentiments, and puts the badges on his army jacket in prominent places.

On Saturday Guy wakes up at sparrowfart, as his father would call it were he not snoring peacefully in his queen-size, which is how Guy has planned it. And once Guy dresses in his sabbing gear he is almost unrecognisable, although of course he can do nothing about the British Bulldog tattoo on his left hand or the one on the other which says DEATH. After which he sneaks downstairs, and within a few minutes is on the road to Chearsley, the village where the hunt is meeting, feeling very pleased with himself and the smooth way things are going.

It is a cool and peaceful morning, and once he gets off the dual carriageway and on to the country lanes there are birds tweeting and cows grazing and baby rabbits hopping in and out of the hedgerows, and Guy walks along enjoying the fresh air and whistling. His only regret is that he does not have his air rifle to liven things up a bit, although in fact it would have the opposite effect on the birds & rabbits etc, as Guy is something of a marksman. But he does not dwell on this thought as he does not wish anything to cast a shadow on his day, but concentrates instead on setting a good pace to Chearsley, with such success that, even allowing for a few refreshment breaks on the way, he makes it in just over an hour.

The result is that he has about three hours before the hunt arrives, and there is nothing in Chearsley it takes three hours to do except waiting for a bus. So after he does a quick recce and checks out the terrain, Guy makes himself comfortable on a convenient bench & opens a can & pulls out his new copy of the Pocket SAS Survival Guide and settles down patiently until things get started.

Nothing much happens for some time, unless you count a couple of old grannies who stagger past and hiss and glare at Guy and mutter things like revolting, but Guy rises above them and continues reading. He is engrossed by a particularly instructive chapter when he hears a kind of baying and yelping, and raises his head to discover he is surrounded by hunt sabs of all shapes and sizes, most of them unimpressive. They are looking at him in a challenging and none-too-friendly way, since it appears that the bench he has chosen is their rallying point and they would like to know what he is doing there.

Guy stands up, which quietens them down a bit, and proceeds to explain in an impassioned manner that he wishes to join them and crush this evil practice of hunting once and for all, and he will kick in anyone's head who tries to stop him. He is able to sound impassioned because he has caught sight of the class A babe, so his voice is trembling with emotion, and at the end of his speech there is a small round of applause and one of the hunt sabs, an earnest sort of person attired in a goatee, steps forward and shakes him by the hand, although he recoils a step when he sees the DEATH tattoo.

'Welcome to the Aylesbury Sabs,' he says. 'We do not let outsiders in as a rule,' and here he looks dubiously at Guy's skinhead haircut. 'But since you have come all this way we are glad to have you aboard,' and other such team-like noises, which make Guy recoil a fraction himself, as he is thinking fondly of the Aylesbury Skins, who would have kicked an outsider's head in first and talked later, or not bothered with the talking part at all.

The Goatee then explains what sabbing is all about, and here Guy almost loses it altogether. It seems that the plan is to wait until the hunt arrives and, after insults are duly exchanged on both sides, the sabs are to run after the hunt and tootle their decoy horns and shout confusing instructions to the dogs, and in this way the fox or whatever will be able to escape in the chaos.

Now even Guy knows that dogs and horses not to mention foxes can run several times faster than even a fit & revved-up hunt sab, which most of this bunch are not, so he does not see that the sabs have an earthly.

'And there is to be no violence,' the Goatee adds mean-ingfully. 'Not even under severe provocation.' Although Guy has only a general idea of what severe provocation is, he is getting the message and not liking it at all. He has a sinking feeling that if anything the hunt will have a good laugh at the sabs and would probably miss their presence if they were not there to spice things up because this is exactly how the Aylesbury Skins once feel about the Aylesbury Mods; indeed all the skins are sad and disappointed when the mods suddenly realise that being a mod is embarrassing and give it up.

It is an uncomfortable sensation for Guy to find himself on the receiving end, and when the hunt arrives he is even more convinced that he has signed up for the wrong team. The hunt and their followers look much fitter and happier than the sabs, also they are swigging out of hip flasks and chaffing with the women around them, all of which Guy feels more at home with than the sabs' thermos flasks and free-range-egg sarnies. But the occasional glimpse of the class A babe sustains him. Besides, the huntsmen are not looking at Guy in a manner which suggests they would welcome his company; on the contrary, they are looking at him in a way which suggests that, after small animals, he is next on their list of items it would be fun to exterminate.

Naturally Guy does not appreciate this at all and his blood begins to rise, especially when the huntsmen begin laughing openly at the sabs and jostling them with their horses and accidentally letting them get in the way of their whips. All the sabs do in return is chant hunting is murder and other such slogans, which do not seem to have much effect on the whole. 'It is pathetic,' Guy tells me, adding that, class A babe or no class A babe, for two pins he would have chucked it then & there.

But he does not, because suddenly there is a tantara and a yoiks and a tally-ho, or whatever huntspeople say, and the hunt gallops off. The sabs and Guy follow in hot pursuit over hill & down dale and so on, which is quite exciting, although the chase cools down a little when a few fields later the sabs reach a large hedge and find that, not having horses, they cannot jump over it.

It is here that Guy really comes into his own. This is despite the fact that, while running alongside the class A babe and trying to make conversation, he is instructed to forget it, since it appears that the class A babe and the Goatee are together & as one and set to remain that way. Of course Guy is heartsore at this news, and indeed for a couple of fields can think of nothing else. But once they reach the hedge he finds he is almost more horrified to discover that the sabs intend to give up and go looking for magic mushrooms instead, on the basis that they are in season and the hunt is doubtless acres away by now.

'For heaven's sake,' Guy tells them, or words to that effect. 'Call yourselves sabs? You cannot give up now. They are bound to come round by that copse over there as it is a dead-cert hang out for foxes,' which he knows because he has shot several in the same copse, although he does not mention it. And he tries to chivvy them up and appeal to their manhoods, and generally sounds like Henry V at Agincourt, and by the end of it many of the sabs are nodding enthusiastically, especially when Guy points out that they would be able to get to the copse first and construct interesting traps and other devices as specified on pages 121-130 of the Pocket SAS Survival Guide.

There is, Guy is surprised to find, still something of a schism in the ranks at his suggestion, the opposition being led by the Goatee and the class A babe, who seem to feel that it is below the belt to resort to such tactics. 'You might hurt someone,' the Goatee keeps saying, and does not appear to be reassured when Guy replies only if the traps work right.

'You might hurt the horses,' the class A babe says even more earnestly, and when Guy shrugs and indicates that the horses take their chances she calls him a butcher and storms off, with the Goatee and a few of the less impressive sabs in tow. And Guy finds he does not care at all, in fact he is is tempted to muse on the fleeting nature of love, but does not as he wishes to try out the deadfall spear trap (p.129).

So Guy leads his sabs to the copse, and they spend a happy forty minutes or so digging pits and tying pieces of mud-smeared rope between trees, although everyone is disappointed to find that building a deadfall spear trap is not practical in the time available. After which they camouflage themselves under piles of leaves and wait, and sure enough there is soon a tantara and the hunt hoves into view over a nearby hill with a small and knackered-looking fox just ahead of it. And the hunt as it gallops into the trees looks fairly splendid, with bright red coats and shiny harrumphing horses and happily baying hounds and so on, but not for long. Because while the hunt might know a thing or two about foxes, the SAS know even more about how to bring a fast-moving object to a sudden stop, and within a matter of seconds there are horses going down like glossy skittles and hounds suddenly finding the path has disappeared from under them, and riders discovering that despite a firm seat in the saddle they are for some reason dangling in mid-air without so much as a stirrup in sight.

In all this chaos it is almost unnecessary for Guy and the other sabs to erupt from their piles of leaves yelling untraditional sab cries along the lines of kill kill kill but they do anyway, with the result that the horses and dogs still standing sensibly decide that they have had enough of this and exit. Guy and the sabs then melt quietly into the trees, although many of them are laughing so hard it is all they can do to walk never mind melt, and Guy takes them to task about this unprofessional behaviour once they have reached a safe distance. It is, however, unanimously agreed that the total score is Sabs 23 Hunt nil, with a rematch planned for the following Saturday.

Guy tells me that he is quietly confident, especially as he has a week to prepare. He has discovered a useful manual in a remaindered bookshop on how soldiers around the world operate in war, containing chapters such as Escape and Evasion in Hostile Territory and Special Forces Personal Protection: Equipped for Battle. But Guy says it all started with the Pocket SAS Survival Guide, and as a result he will treasure it for ever.

And he seems to forget completely about the ICF, except to say in passing that this new hobby makes them look like the WI. So all in all it is a good thing Guy's father gives him the Pocket SAS Survival Guide for his birthday, though as Guy's father is an avid hunt supporter and is planning to follow them himself next Saturday, it is possible he will not think so.

THREE

Thanks to a small private clinic in Oxford, Dave the builder becomes Doris the builder, and although the transformation actually takes place some weeks before, Doris does not previously feel up to celebrating it much. But it seems all is now well and settling into place, and so Guy & I find ourselves observing Doris celebrating in style by giving away free bevvies all night at the Bell in Aylesbury.

Many of Doris's building friends and acquaintances are gathered to mark the passing of Dave the builder's wedding tackle, and not all of them are there for the free drinks. Dave the builder stands six foot seven in his socks and Doris is not noticeably smaller, also she still boasts the slablike biceps and meaty fists of which Dave is formerly so proud, not to mention his temper, so naturally enough her fellow builders do not like to risk offence by refusing. The beer is therefore flowing like lager, and though at first Doris's friends and acquaintances seem unsure whether to call Doris him or her, this problem is rapidly resolved when Doris headbutts someone for using the former, so everyone else is able to relax. And the only sour note is struck by Malcolm the landlord, who objects thoroughly to Doris, mainly on principle but also because Doris's dress sense runs to black string vests with no bra and mini-skirts with g-string knickers, and does even when she is still Dave.

Malcolm has therefore never gone a bundle on Dave in the first place, and it looks like he is not about to alter his opinion, because despite her new sex Doris is not behaving like a lady at all. Indeed, she is swigging pints and slapping her impressive beer belly and offering to display her new chest, of which she is understandably proud, and telling indelicate jokes very loudly, at which everyone else laughs heartily, even if privately they do not find them at all amusing.

But Malcolm is looking increasingly surly, and after Doris tells the one about how do you get a nun pregnant, Malcolm goes to a telephone behind the bar and makes a few phone calls to some acquaintances of his own, in which Doris is mentioned several times, and always with gritted teeth. Which does not look good for Doris the builder as, although Malcolm is a leading light of the Aylesbury Rotarians, not to mention a member of the church council, he has several even more unpleasant connections and quite a few people suspect he is not a forgiving person at all, despite his religion.

Pretty soon Guy & I get up to leave, having a dinner engagement down the chinky. On seeing this, Doris is shouting what is your problem in a challenging way, as is her wont; but we rise above it, being used to Dave behaving in this general fashion anyway. As a result we miss the rest of Doris's evening, but it seems that, while we are having a pleasant and civilised time at the Golden Dragon, Doris is having an increasingly wild one at the Bell, concluding with her armwrestling two builders at once and forgetting to pay for the damage when she finally leaves. Although this is an understand-able omission, it no doubt contributes to Malcolm's satisfaction when he thinks of what is coming to Doris while he picks up the pieces & sweeps up his tables and otherwise closes up for the night.

It is a cold and starry evening, and Doris is staggering away from the Bell with her building friends, singing Frigging in the Rigging in a rousing way, as she is not sober. And her building friends are dutifully intoning good on yer Doris, and Doris is replying emotionally that they are all mates, and what are mates for? when they round a corner and come to a sudden stop. Because in the middle of the pavement, surrounded by several of his larger companions, is local garage proprietor Sean Devizes, who is also known to be one of Malcolm's closer associates. And although Doris starts shouting what is your problem and threatening to bare her chest, her voice soon trails off as it is obvious that Sean and his companions are not interested in badinage, but are pulling out knuckledusters and bike chains from their pockets in a businesslike manner.

Even through her haze Doris can see they are up to no good, and being not averse to violence she is swinging her arms around and pumping her biceps up and looking at her building friends, saying got a bit of a situation here boys, and thinking to herself it will be a laugh. But Sean looks hard at Doris, then turns to his sidekicks and says, 'What is that?'

And his sidekicks shrug & seem not to have the answer, though there are many unkind suggestions, but the general consensus appears to be that whatever it is would benefit from some readjustment, at which point they begin to move forward.

Doris cannot believe her ears. She has never experienced this attitude in her life; on the contrary, no one has even dared comment on her appearance, let alone be offensive about it. However, she is not a coward, and although somewhat shocked and upset, she turns to her building friends saying, 'No one gets away with that,' in decisive tones.

*　　*　　*

But it seems that they do, because in the time it takes for Sean and his companions to move in, most of the building friends have done a runner and Doris sees to her surprise that there are only a couple left. She is touched and grateful all the same, and says as much, at which her building friends snigger and shout to Sean and his companions, 'Go on, it's about time someone did,' after which they too depart at top speed.

There follows a huge scrum in which Doris finds herself acting as the ball, and although she puts up a pretty good fight she does not really stand a chance, since a boot soon catches her on the back of the neck and she lapses into unconsciousness and knows no more. Under the circumstances this is a good thing, because her attackers do not stop there. In fact they continue with increased enthusiasm, and if the comments they are making are not pleasant, neither is what they are doing with their knuckledusters & bike chains etc.

Finally everyone stops for a break, the only question in their minds being whether they should finish off on the spot or put Doris in the boot of a car and continue elsewhere. There is a bit of debate, and opinion is wavering towards the second option, as this would allow extra time with Doris in a more private setting, when all of a sudden the night is shattered by the ner-ner-ner-ner of a siren, and everyone says fuck and run for it, realising that one of the passers by must have performed their christian duty and phoned for the police.

Eventually a panda car screeches round the corner in time to find the street deserted. It is just about to screech off again when there is a loud groaning sound and the noise of creaking bones, and a huge, blood-stained figure in a ripped string vest rises from the pavement and staggers towards it. It is an unnerving sight, especially as somewhere along the line Doris has been relieved of her mini-skirt and g-string, and one of the officers, who is young and new to the area, says fuck and coincidentally also urges his partner to run for it. But the other officer is sucking his truncheon thoughtfully and looking at the figure, and coming slowly to the conclusion that there are not many six-foot-seven women built like brick outhouses in Aylesbury. So he says tentatively, 'Doris?' at which the figure makes burbling noises indicative of agreement and lurches towards them with outstretched arms.

The next thing Doris knows is that she is in one of Aylesbury's police cells with a few extra truncheon-shaped bruises, and a couple of boys in blue are standing outside the cell discussing her in loud voices. For a horrible moment Doris thinks she is back on the pavement as the gist of their conversation is not much different to the conversation there. If anything it is worse, because she has previously had a romantic view of the police, and has often said that the government should put more of them on the street. And she has always voted conservative and been careful not to cause any trouble when the police are around, so as not to add to their workload. So the revelation that they also think she is a freak & a sideshow is a harsh one.

Thus Doris is crushed & disheartened, and is even grateful when a passing duty sergeant throws her a pair of old trousers, explaining that she is turning his stomach. And the next morning she is informed that she is free to go, providing of course she has no complaints. Doris humbly says that she has none, which seems to disappoint some of the policemen, and then she says that she thinks she had better leave as she has to tell work she will be off sick for a couple of days. No one says oh no, must you be going so soon, so in minutes she finds herself on the street and limping slowly towards her flat.

Her vision is still blurred and shaking and she is having to squint even more because it is a bright day, but she cannot help noticing people giggling as she passes, and others are crossing the street to avoid her, and when a group of schoolboys starts shouting got a good kicking then Doris? and so on she realises that word has somehow got around. Although the weather is sunny Doris is feeling colder and colder, and by the time she rings work she is not astonished to hear that her presence is no longer required and she will get a week in lieu.

For the rest of the day Doris holes up in her flat doing some hard and painful thinking about her future, and much of her past life & assertive behaviour is also flashing in front of her eyes although she is not drowning. And later on that evening, a huge and bedraggled figure clutching a battered old vinyl suitcase and wearing one of its least revealing mini-skirts climbs on the train from Aylesbury to London, and that is the last anyone sees of Doris for some time.

A few months later the community are in Anna's caff, which is fairly buzzing with gossip. Every new person through the door comes up to the table asking whether they have heard about the Bell, and the table replies that of course it has, indeed they are already discussing the subject. But it is clear that no one really knows anything, except that the Bell is closed until the company finds a new landlord, owing to Malcolm the landlord having mysteriously disappeared.

The only person remaining aloof from all this is Guy, who says he despises gossip. He is looking out of the window and pretending to be fascinated by the sights of Aylesbury High St, when all at once he stiffens and lets out a thoughtful whistle.

Since drawing up outside the caff is a huge gold-painted old rolls complete with tinted windows & whitewall tyres. As soon as it slides to a halt the door opens, after which a long leg wrapped in black fishnet emerges, followed by a view of someone Guy accurately describes at the time as a stunner, although he insists later that he is referring to the rolls. The stunner has wavy blonde hair and bright red lippy and carefully applied blusher, and is wearing a little black suit which curves in and out in an interesting way. Several of the men across the street pause and are eyeing her up in an unsubtle manner, but they move on fairly rapidly after the stunner continues to unfold from the car long after everyone expects her to stop, and it becomes apparent that she could have three of them for breakfast, always supposing she would want to.

No one expects her to come into the caff, although several of the male members of the community are crossing their fingers and muttering silent prayers. But whatever they are praying to must listen, because the door opens, and the stunner slinks in and Anna rushes out from behind her counter and shouts, 'Doris.' And Doris grins a wide grin and does not deny it at which everyone is struck dumb with amazement, mingled with a certain amount of disquiet at the thought they are all fancying her more than anything.

Anna sits her down and fusses over her in a motherly mediterranean way, saying she should have written, but to show there are really no hard feelings she brings Doris her special coffee, which Doris gallantly starts drinking. Then Anna sits down and says expectantly, 'Well, Doris?'

Doris informs her that it is Dolores now, actually, but that Anna can call her Doris if she wishes, as she will never forget what Anna has done for her. And the rest of the caff hears that, before Doris does her runner, she phones Anna, who has a notorious soft spot for women of more than average height, being not exactly petite herself. And Doris throws herself on Anna's mercy, after which Anna not only coughs up fifty quid and an old London A-Z, but also gives her the number of a distant cousin who runs a temping agency and might be able to put something Doris's way.

Doris is extremely grateful and hugs Anna with tears in her eyes and other unusual signs of emotion, and when Anna says this must mean she is a reformed character, Doris manages a watery smile and sets off for the station with her head held higher than before, although not much higher as her neck is still killing her.

The train journey is uneventful, and by the time she pulls into Victoria Doris is feeling much refreshed and up to ringing Anna's distant cousin, who she is hoping will maybe offer her a bed for the night. But after sticking her 10p in the slot she hears a colourless voice saying welcome, you have reached the offices of Soho Saints, the temping agency for all your requirements, opening hours nine till five, please leave a message. And Doris accidentally leaves a message saying fuck, and then she bangs the receiver against the wall, as she is not all that reformed and it is already 9pm.

Nevertheless she pulls herself together and limps gamely round Victoria until she finds a small guest house called Bougainvillea Heights, and in no time at all the sound of snoring is drowning out the noise of traffic and car alarms and shouting and breaking glass from outside. And bright and early the next morning Doris is in Soho, looking around her with some disappointment as she cannot see a single prostitute, although there are many media executives enjoying breakfast cappuccinos outside street cafés to replace them.

The execs are returning her surprised look and then some, since even in London Doris cuts a striking figure, and would do so even were she not giving the impression of having dived head-first into a waste disposal unit, thanks to Sean and his companions. All things considered, the reaction of Anna's distant cousin when Doris enters Soho Saints is quite understandable, though Doris feels it is unprofessional of her to scream, and says as much.

Once Anna's distant cousin calms down a bit, although she still looks as though she wishes she were even more distant, possibly by a mile or so, she shuffles some papers and says, much as she would like to help, she can think of nothing suitable, as she does not see Doris fitting in as a receptionist in a merchant bank, and that is the kind of job she has on her books. She says this extremely firmly, and gets up and says that she is sorry but Doris has to leave now, and she does this so smoothly that Doris is standing on the pavement before she realises that she did not want to leave at all, as she has not the faintest idea what to do next.

Anna, who is listening to Doris's story with many encouraging nods and little interjections, now gets up in fury and begins to pace around the caff saying, 'I never liked her side of the family, would you like me to send the boys round one night Doris, it is the least I can do.'

Doris replies soothingly that there is no need, and that actually this turns out to be the best thing that could have happened, not that she realises it at the time. In fact at the time she sinks down on to the pavement and, although decades of conditioning as Dave the builder prevent her from sobbing hysterically, she is not far off it. When suddenly a voice pierces through her misery, and the voice is saying, 'Move, you bitch, can't you? Oh for heaven's sake, move.'

At first Doris assumes that the voice is talking to her, as

she is getting quite used to this sort of thing by now, but when she looks up she sees a very plump, oldish bloke dressed in a skin tight lycra biking outfit, wrestling furiously with the lock on the door of a building behind her, and it looks like the lock is winning. Doris is feeling in the need of some human contact, also she knows about locks and things thanks to her building experience, so she limps over and asks if she can help in any way. And the plump bloke, instead of screaming or recoiling or anything, says, 'Oh, could you be a sweetheart, I would be eternally grateful. I have to rehearse for tonight, and if I don't get in it will be such an enormous disaster I can't tell you.'

But while Doris is talking persuasively to the lock and gently jiggling the key around in it, the bloke tells her a lot. It turns out that the door belongs to a club called Madame Jo Jo's, and the bloke is the compère of the singing and dancing extravaganza for which Madame Jo Jo's is world famous. And after Doris sweet-talks the lock into opening and is feeling quite pleased with herself the bloke grabs her by the hand and says, 'Delicia Delight, eternally in your debt.' And Doris automatically says Dave, pleased to meet you, and then realises her mistake and blushes and says I mean Doris.

At which Delicia Delight looks her up and down, which takes some time as there is a lot of Doris, and asks if she would like a coffee before he starts. Doris gratefully agrees, thinking to herself that she has never come across anyone like Delicia Delight in her life, and feeling rather strange about the fact that if she had come across him back in Aylesbury she would have called him many unpleasant names before running him out of town with the help of her building friends. But instead she finds herself telling Delicia Delight the story of her own flight from Aylesbury over a cappuccino. She does not try to make herself look good in any way, and admits that she probably had it coming, to which Delicia Delight agrees, but kindly. Doris explains that she has always wanted to be a woman, so she is not exactly sure why she is still behaving like a builder, and Delicia Delight says it is probably protective colouration, as Aylesbury sounds like the kind of place where someone like Doris would need it.

By the third cappuccino Doris is gazing at Delicia Delight with dog-like devotion, so when he looks at his watch and screams oh my god, my rehearsal, her ears droop in misery. And her tail, if she had one, would be clamped between her legs, and she thinks about begging but is too proud. So when Delicia Delight says come on, sweetie, what are you waiting for, we need a new bouncer as the last one was a nightmare, and you can stay over at my place until you get yourself sorted, Doris nearly rolls over in delight, but mutters, 'Thanks,' instead.

A couple of days later, once her bruises have gone

down, Doris is installed at the door of Madame Jo Jo's in an outsized, sequinned evening dress and having a breeze, as when the customers see a six-foot-seven female bouncer they are impressed and amazed and give no trouble at all, even when Doris has to turn many of them away. Because Doris discovers that Madame Jo Jo's is a popular venue even among people like bankers and so on. She is surprised by this, since despite the fact that the waitresses may look like glamorous & desirable females, they are not. And the floor show also consists of men impersonating the other side, including Delicia Delight, together with some very butch fellows in minuscule costumes who dance in a suggestive way and who, Delicia Delight says, are really there for the staff to enjoy, though the punters seem to like them too, especially the bankers.

And although it is all done in the best possible taste Doris has difficulty getting her Aylesbury head round it, but she sensibly decides to relax & enjoy, and as a result becomes very popular with all the staff, who consider her an asset to the club and are always popping round to her new flat with plants and so on to make her feel at home. On top of that, the waitresses give her tips on dressing and hairstyles and what colour lippy to wear, and Doris discovers that a recreational drug such as cocaine is not only more entertaining than lager, but makes her lose weight at a satisfying rate, though she knows this is not a diet recommended by doctors.

Weeks pass, and Doris has almost blanked Aylesbury out altogether, and is talking knowledgeably about clubbing and restaurants and moaning about the tube as if she were a Londoner born & bred. And when Delicia Delight asks her if she would ever go back Doris says not likely, even though she has occasional revenge fantasies about Sean and his companions, and especially Malcolm, because she has put two and two together and concluded that the companions were not outside the Bell that evening by chance.

One night Doris has just broken up a fight between two of her admirers, and has seen them off with some relief. Even though one of them is a lawyer and the other a producer for Channel 4, and both are flatteringly keen & eager, she still feels nervous about dating. Delicia Delight keeps telling her to take the plunge, and says that personally he would have either of them like a shot, preferably both; but Doris maintains that she is not yet ready, at which Delicia Delight tuts and says some people just do not know their luck.

It is getting late and the show is almost over, and Doris feels the need for a bevvy. So she hands over door duty to her new deputy, and is sipping a vodka, lime & soda at her specially reserved table, when Mike the head waitress comes up to her saying, 'We have a problem on table three. I cannot imagine why Alan let them in.'

Doris looks up with professional interest and then chokes on her vod because who is sitting at table three but Malcolm, together with Sean and all their companions. They all look as though they have had nine or ten over the eight, and are gulping down yet more whisky and beer, and from their behaviour they have not realised the nature of the club at all. They are leering at all the waitresses and groping them as they pass and shouting get them out darling, unaware that none of the waitresses has anything to get out, and that what they are leering at is just clever padding and blusher artfully applied as shading. And Malcolm is behaving the worst of all and not at all like a member of the church council or even the Rotary Club, indeed several of the waitresses are glaring at him with hatred as he is drooling & manhandling them and yelling this is the life lads, we should have done this years ago.

Mike asks hopefully what Doris is planning, knowing that her usual style would be to throw them out, and not gently. But Doris beckons him closer and whispers in his ear. Within a second Mike is reeling back with surprise, as everyone working in the club has heard about Malcolm etc from Delicia Delight and Mike cannot believe that they are there. 'But what are you going to do?' he says again with more trepidation, and Doris beckons him even closer and whispers some more, after which Mike claps his hands in glee and goes off to pass the word round.

Backstage, Delicia Delight is changing out of his spangled tutu and getting ready to go home, and failing to take one of the butchest dancers home with him, but when he hears the news he cheers up no end and calls all the other dancers into his dressing room for a confab. And when all the waitresses hear what is up they go into little knots and start giggling, and then start hustling the other customers out of the club like skilled sheepdogs.

Soon table three is the only table left, and they do not notice, as they are distracted by the arrival of a magnum of free champagne with compliments from Dolores, who of course is Doris, although they do not know it. In fact, when Doris sashays up to them saying huskily, 'Let's drink to each other, boys,' their tongues hang out and their eyes bulge, and they knock back the champagne at 90mph while Doris smiles sweetly at them even though she does not feel sweet at all.

Having swigged his champagne down, Malcolm stands up and staggers towards Doris with outstretched arms, gurgling how about a dance? and not appearing to realise that there is no music playing. But to his bemusement the figure of Doris is receding in a strange and disturbing way, as is the rest of the room, and two seconds later he is kissing the carpet and out for the count, because the champagne contains a preparation of Delicia Delight's which he describes as a Mickey

Finn Plus and keeps in the club medicine cabinet for emergencies.

The companions have just enough time to say what and er before their heads dive on to the table, and by prodding and poking them the waitresses ascertain that they too are out cold. So they shout ready, and the dancers appear and carry Malcolm and the companions on to the stage, where they have laid out a fascinating array of props ranging from whips and bondage corsets and chains and dog collars, which are used in the show, to giant black dildos and arm-length black rubber gloves, which are not, and Delicia Delight says he cannot think where they come from, and winks.

Doris asks if they will really need all that stuff, and Delicia Delight replies that he really thinks they will. He adds that if Doris is squeamish she doesn't have to stay, and Doris muses for a bit and then says that she thinks she ought to stay, just to keep an eye on things.

And in no time at all Malcolm and his companions are stripped down to their essentials and their trousers and shirts are replaced by more quirky attire, and the staff are arranging them in all sorts of interesting poses, many of which they would probably find extremely painful and intrusive were they not unconscious. The staff, however, are enjoying themselves thoroughly, and making full use of all props etc until eventually Delicia

Delight says with some regret that he thinks they had better call it a night, as his Mickey Finn Plus will be wearing off before too long.

An hour or so later, Malcolm and his companions find themselves waking up in a dark Soho alleyway, dressed in their shirts and trousers. Their first thought is that they have all been mugged, but as they try to stand up they are all wondering exactly what sort of mugging would leave them feeling quite so tender in so many intimate places, and the next thing that happens is that Malcolm looks down and sees hundreds of polaroid photos scattered on the alley floor, which naturally he picks up. But he throws them down again, quivering with horror and unable to believe his eyes, because the polaroid photos are of him and his companions on stage at Madame Jo Jo's. Many of the pictures are close-ups, and all of them are in glorious technicolour, and they would all be banned under the Obscene Publications Act. And Malcolm and his companions have equal expressions of disgust and nausea on their faces, and none of them dare to look at each other; instead they scrabble around until they have picked up all the photos and hastily leave in opposite directions, although it is noticeable that all of them are walking rather strangely, and several appear to be in shock.

As Malcolm staggers down the alley going he knows not where, he is thinking that at least this will not get around as none of the companions will ever talk, and he most certainly will not. And although his social life will be severely curtailed, since he never wants to see any of his companions again, having apparently seen so much of them recently, he reckons things could be worse.

And he is right, and they are much worse. And the caff and Anna, who are getting earache from all this listening, now discover the solution to the mystery of why Malcolm has suddenly disappeared off Aylesbury's social scene altogether, and why he will never be coming back.

Because on putting his hand into his trouser pocket Malcolm discovers a piece of scented pink notepaper. And the note says, 'Just thought you should know I have sent the best photos to the church council and the Rotary Club.' And it is signed, 'Your old mate Doris.' And then it says, 'PS. I never knew you had it in you.'

Which Doris admits is a cheap & unnecessary pun, but no one in the caff blames her for not resisting it.

F O U R

It is Monday or possibly Tuesday evening, and I am wandering across Aylesbury's market square which is vacant as usual, and thinking of David Bowie's song Five Years, and humming it to myself. It is not a particularly good song, but it is nevertheless interesting for anyone living in Aylesbury, because Bowie claims to be referring to this very square in the line 'Pushing through the market square,' and I therefore conclude that he must be referring to a Saturday, when things are generally busier.

Now for once I am not concerning myself about business, having recently taken on a partner. This is none other than my old acquaintance Guy, who is at leisure ever since his father discovers his sabbing tendencies and calls him a viper in his bosom & a disgrace to the family trade and sacks him. And the business is now showing a healthy profit, because through sheer force of personality Guy is encouraging all our customers to pay up on time, if not before, also ever since Guy exerts his personality on Mick-ther-man's associate, he seems to fade from the picture. So all in all things are looking up & settling down nicely.

I am making my way to the Kings Head, which I am reserving for pleasure not business, the Kings Head being an antique & popular resort frequented by all and sundry including Aylesbury's forces of law & order, particularly the undercover versions. Although these are coming in many guises, such as ties or sweaters and so on, even the most unobservant members of the community are penetrating the camouflage and saving their bad habits for more private venues. As a result, the forces of law & order spend a great deal of time propped against the bar sporting disappointed expressions, and presumably they are wondering why the view is so uninspiring, but since the community get to do whatever they enjoy elsewhere, and the forces of law are left free & untroubled and well supplied with expense-account pints, it is widely agreed to be a convenient arrangement all round.

So I am approaching the Kings Head doors when I am distracted by the sight of an old VW beetle which is crawling round the square like a tortoise. To my surprise I see it contains a parent & daughter set known as Miranda & her mother, who are not on display since way back, indeed during the days when the community are still young & fresh & innocent, or at any rate more so. Currently the beetle is displaying a little sticker saying I Brake for Children, which is reassuring, and Miranda's mother appears to be tossing back her head and laughing gaily, as does Miranda, and these sights are most unsettling, since back in the old days Miranda & her mother are something of a three-act tragedy, and chances are Miranda will be laughing gaily only if her mother is discovered under a beetle rather than inside it.

Since at the time, along with the rest of Miranda's family, Miranda's mother is what is often described as a little eccentric, though Miranda herself is calling a spade a spade and her nearest & dearest barking. But while her old father is for years safely tucked away in a high-security rest home, and her big brother is making only infrequent home visits, during which he is seen taking a vodka bottle for walks on the end of a piece of string, Miranda is forced to live cheek-to-cheek with her mother, on account of poverty & age and so on, and they are therefore as sisters, though not the loving sort.

Indeed at the time Miranda is always insisting she will take menopausal Simon's mother as a straight swap, menopausal Simon being a community member who acquires his name through having a face like a sunset, if not as poetic. And all the men who hear this think it most strange, since menopausal Simon's mother is an old person closely resembling her son & heir, while Miranda's mother is something of a first-round knockout, and in fact visions of Miranda's mother are disturbing their youthful rest on more than one occasion. On top of this, Miranda's mother's eccentric behaviour is seemingly of the tasteful sort, in that she rarely comes out except late at night, and then only to wander the grounds in a white-clad & see-through fashion.

Of course the men think this most romantic, and to start with are appearing very friendly & pally towards Miranda in the hopes of getting a front-row seat. But Miranda is showing no inclination to dispense tickets. Were she any other female the chances are she would be discarded on the spot, since in those days the community are not interesting themselves in females beyond the basics. But instead everyone contents themselves with the occasional glimpse of Miranda's mother from afar, and when Miranda is present are showing tact beyond their years and dropping the subject. Because in the mean time Miranda reveals herself as a sensible & practical type with a forthright manner and a high tolerance for guinness, and as a result is soon being held in much esteem by the male contingent, who indeed are adopting her as a brother.

But one day Miranda is to reveal herself as one hundred

per cent female, and this unpleasant discovery naturally
occurs down the Kings Head, where the gathering are
annexing their usual table and turning their thoughts
to the following Friday, this being the date a singer is
coming to town. Singers and similar are often coming to
the civic hall, which engagement they use as something
of a practice session, and most Fridays there is a minor
band on stage, saying hello Aylesbury in tones of dejection
before they depart on their real tour and more glamorous
locations, such as Birmingham.

Although this particular singer is reaching over the hill
and almost down the other side, he is widely considered
a catch for Aylesbury, since many people recognise his
name, even if they are not able to remember exactly
what he does with it. Indeed it seems he has been out
of fame & circulation for some time, and so Eddie the
civic manager is walking like a pigeon in triumph at
booking Trevor Smith's comeback performance, Trevor
Smith being the singer's original title which early on
he discards. And every lamppost in the area is boasting a poster saying The Civic Presents Trevor Smith
Live, which the older generation are apparently pleased
& surprised to hear about, though naturally the community are none too bothered either way.

So the table is turning to other matters, when Miranda
heaves a mournful sigh but otherwise remains unnaturally silent. It transpires that all along she is nursing a

dark & painful secret, which the community eventually hears with some disbelief, since she discloses that, ever since she is just a little schoolgirl in braces, she has a crush on or passion for none other than Trevor Smith. And as she gets older if not wiser, her girlish fantasies develop around meeting him and finding they are designed for each other, as, Miranda points out, ageing rock stars and young females so often are. As a result she is feeling a little aggrieved to hear her idol dismissed in the above fashion.

The gathering start to wish they had never asked what was on Miranda's mind in the first place, and are eyeing menopausal Simon with some disfavour, he having originally placed the question. But as soon as they hear that Miranda is planning to attend Friday's performance they supportively assure her she will not be alone, and look most virtuous when she reacts to this offer with suspicion, saving any hilarity and so on until she exits.

So Friday night duly arrives, and Miranda enters the Kings Head for a pre-concert bevvy as arranged. Many jaws drop & there are more swallows than spring, because Miranda seems to have forgotten most of her clothing, and what she has on looks to have shrunk, and although she is looking more female than anyone has ever predicted, the set of her chin deters any comment.

The gathering proceed to the civic, where everyone is

shortly clutching bevvies and watching Trevor Smith make his debut. And Trevor Smith is prancing and kicking up his heels in a fashion which has many people wondering if he has consulted a doctor about this activity beforehand, although there are several cries of hurrah and so on from other areas. But gradually these die away and the floor starts murmuring with unease, as Trevor Smith stops his cavorting and settles down to singing, and he is revealed to sound more like a drain than a person, although he seems not to notice and continues moaning & gargling into his microphone with great conviction. And presently his audience are casting down their plastic glasses and leaving in droves, and by the time Trevor Smith tells Aylesbury he loves it, and sensibly exits without waiting to hear if this emotion is reciprocated, the hall is like a vacuum.

But the community is left standing among the debris and shuffling, since half-way through Trevor Smith's performance Miranda has disappeared. Everyone is wondering whether to mount a rescue or search party when a side door opens and Trevor Smith emerges, and behind him, flushed with pride & achievement, is Miranda.

Now Trevor Smith is scanning the area in the manner of a man searching for groupies, and when he sees the assembled and unwomanly gathering his face drops and his chins sag and he looks on the verge of retreat, though no further, as Miranda is blocking it. But Miranda tells

him, 'These are your greatest fans,' at which Trevor
Smith seems to brighten a little, and the gathering
suddenly find themselves clutching Trevor Smith auto-
graphs & Trevor Smith T-shirts & the Trevor Smith
comeback single, and although they are soon laden
down with these items no one is feeling at all indebted,
as Trevor Smith still appears to have a shopload to spare.

So they are still reeling from this shock when Miranda
suggests repairing elsewhere for a party, but it seems
that Trevor Smith's hotel is out of bounds, owing to a
travelling companion or secretary he is keeping in his
bedroom. But Miranda declares that this is no problem,
since everyone can go back to her desirable residence.
And just before she herds Trevor Smith into a taxi she
instructs everyone else to keep her mother occupied on
arrival, after which Miranda & Trevor Smith vanish in a
puff of exhaust smoke.

For a moment or so the gathering is standing stunned, but
within seconds they are recovering and leaping into a
nearby capri, of which Guy is the proud if not entirely
legal owner, and once everyone fits in and on top of
each other, the capri is rapidly heading in the general
direction of Nether Winchendon, this being the small
and otherwise uninspiring village where Miranda lives.

Now this capri is a popular vehicle, being generally
full of illegal substances, and after about ten minutes

it is significantly less full due to everyone being in a party spirit. It is therefore an interesting if somewhat hazardous journey. At one point the capri overtakes the taxi, where it slows down enough for everyone to remark that Miranda & Trevor Smith do not seem to be talking at all; instead, Trevor Smith is attacking Miranda like an ice-cream, and Miranda is showing no attempt to preserve her wrappings, and so after a while the capri continues tactfully on its way until it reaches Miranda's village.

By this stage the capri is full of empty wraps and spliff-ends and bits of pill-sized clingfilm, and for some time it motors around visiting many cottages and asking if they belong to Miranda. Invariably they do not, and their inhabitants seem not inclined to help, several hinting they are more inclined to dial 999 even though this would not be helpful at all. But by this process of elimination the capri eventually arrives at Miranda's place, which turns out to be a forbidding & crumbling old place in the Gothic style, so everyone makes horror noises and then they fall out of the car.

The taxi draws up, and Miranda & Trevor Smith emerge in a somewhat dishevelled state, and the gathering are saying shush quite loudly so as not to disturb Miranda's mother, when the front door opens to reveal a figure outlined in the light of the hallway.

*   *   *

And the gathering are left unmanned, and also wishing they had not indulged quite so much in the capri, being less able to focus than they are wanting. Because the figure is wearing a blank expression, and not much else other than a floaty white caftan, and Miranda is saying oh no in fury, because as soon as Trevor Smith spots this figure his nose is pointing towards it like a setter's. No matter how much Miranda tugs at his arm and adjusts her cleavage and so on, Trevor Smith soon seems to have forgotten her existence.

Finally Miranda's mother's gaze roams round the driveway and settles on Trevor Smith. At which view her lips slowly part company, and she says in somewhat blurred tones, 'Trevor.' Trevor Smith winces as if in pain, since he is normally referred to as Brett or similar, and after a moment or so says, 'Yes?' in tones of obvious doubt and with no visible pleasure.

Miranda's mother appears to be wishing to add something, but whatever it is it is not coming out, so she starts to sway instead and retreats into the hallway. Miranda, now a shade of pink, is examining the ground, as it is clear to all & sundry that her mother is in the grip of some strong emotion or, alternatively, spirits.

And Trevor Smith is saying what is this? in obvious disenchantment, and looking around for Guy as a potential chauffeur, the taxi having long since departed. But Guy is propped up against a flowerbed and murmuring what idiot put that step there, someone could fall over it to himself, and it is obvious that he is in no condition to drive anything and probably would not be even if he were upright.

Miranda suggests that Trevor Smith had better phone for a taxi, and follows him into the house with the determined air of a person about to cut the wires, and after some consultation the rest of the gathering pick up Guy and follow suit. Inside there is no sign of Miranda or her mother, though from the cursing & cries of tomorrow? it seems that Trevor Smith is still trying to find transport. So everyone settles down in a nearby room, and a strong, herbal aroma is soon wafting through the air.

After what seems an age, Miranda's mother enters looking somewhat distraught and wishing to know when anyone has last seen her daughter. The gathering spring courteously to their feet, reassuringly Miranda is bound to turn up any minute, since they are enjoying the sight of Miranda's mother more than a little, and do not wish to lose it again. Close up, she does not disappoint, being well preserved to the point of being pickled, and although she is clutching a vacant bottle in one hand and an unlit cig in another it does not seem to diminish her charms at all.

Indeed, when Miranda's mother proves unreliable on

her feet and has to reach out for support there is no shortage of takers, though personally I remain unmoved. On reflection I am unmoved throughout the entire evening, being somewhat surprised to find myself present in the first place, and this is possibly owing to experiences I have enjoyed the night before, although I cannot seem to remember these either.

However, thanks to the fresh country air or whatever I am at least on my feet and able to take in my surroundings, and currently Miranda's mother is standing with a set look on her features, while in front of her menopausal Simon is doing nineteen or possibly twenty to the dozen and regaling her with many amusing anecdotes & personal experiences, this being the danger of indulging in stimulants. And Miranda's mother appears to have given up any hope of getting a syllable in edgeways, and is not looking happy at all. She makes several concerted efforts to cross the room and exit, but every time she finds her route blocked by one member of the gathering or another, and no matter how determined she is to escape, they are invariably more determined and will not let her. And after having her every attempt foiled, and being forced to listen to everyone in turn, Miranda's mother appears to sag and give in, and ends up sucking with desperation on any can or bottle going.

Now I am feeling like testing my legs, so I leave Miranda's mother in the tender care of whoever and begin exploring the hallway. In my mind is a kitchen, and possibly a can or two somewhere inside it. It is while I am thus engaged that I pass a small room which is filled with the sound of sucking and other strange noises, and on cautiously opening the door I am greeted by the sight of Trevor Smith & Miranda.

Trevor Smith is currently behaving in a most maidenly way, and wriggling and voicing protest, but Miranda's chin wears a determined expression I recognise of old, and she is saying relax in dulcet tones, which are not seeming to have any effect except the opposite. Meanwhile Trevor Smith is gazing over her shoulder with a hunted air about him, when suddenly he catches my eye and leaps to his feet saying look, we have company like a man grabbing a lifeline.

But Miranda greets me with a face like a bottle of poison. I am happy to take the hint, but Trevor Smith says no no, we can keep it for later, and pulls a bag out of his pocket with enthusiasm, after which he proceeds to chase the dragon with sighs of relief. I am disapproving, owing to smack being a very suspect drug and one which I would never touch, so I wander in, although not in time to stop Miranda inhaling in an amateur & defiant manner. Afterwards she starts to look very ill, and departs to recover.

But then Trevor Smith begins talking from his corner,

and persists in his conversation, which mainly concerns Trevor Smith and how stressful it is to be a star & idol and how I have no idea what the pressures are like, which, it is true, I do not. Finally I make my excuses and escape back to the main room, where I find that Guy has come round and is taking his turn with Miranda's mother. Menopausal Simon is meanwhile complaining that Guy forfeited his turn by being unconscious, while Guy is holding him off with an outstretched arm and continuing to talk at Miranda's mother who is now looking increasingly tormented.

So I am nearly on my way out again, and wondering if my system is up to this constant motion when there is a slight interruption, caused by Miranda entering the room in a manner no one can fail to notice, i.e. she walks in and falls over, and although she picks herself up pretty quickly all eyes are now upon her, which she probably regrets as she looks like death.

Miranda's mother, seeing her daughter white-faced and sweating and falling out of what few clothes she has on, seems to sober rapidly and bolts across the room saying, 'Miranda What has he done to you?'

'Nothing', says Miranda, and her mother sags with relief; but Miranda has not finished. 'Nothing, I mean,' she continues, 'that I didn't want him to do.' And she looks at her parent in a challenging fashion.

The room is now quiet as a grave, apart from the gathering shushing each other so they can hear better, so it is into an unearthly silence that Miranda proudly announces, 'It was beautiful.'

It is only weeks later that I wonder when Trevor Smith has had the time to fit Miranda in, beautifully or otherwise, but at the time I do not question her statement, and neither does Miranda's mother. Instead she screams as though she has just been shot. And everyone looks more than a little puzzled, as no one can work out whether she is filled with envy or simply objecting to Trevor Smith as a potential son-in-law, but either way the feeling is that she is going somewhat over the top about it.

But when Miranda discloses that Trevor Smith has invited her on tour with him, starting tomorrow, it is obviously the last straw because Miranda's mother collapses as if her back has given way, and Miranda runs out accompanied by many hysterical sobs and disappears into the night.

The gathering are taking this as a hint that the party is over, and are stepping hastily over Miranda's mother and fleeing for the capri, barely pausing to say thanks and what a pleasant evening and so on, but Guy & I notice that Miranda's mother is still comatose among the spliff-ends. Naturally we do not wish to leave her in this state, so in the end we carry her upstairs, and while we are laying her tenderly on a bed she begins muttering Miranda, Miranda to herself, and Guy & I tell her that everything is fine, and she says no it is not. So Guy says cheeringly that Trevor Smith is not that bad a person, even though he is possibly old enough to be Miranda's father, and here he grinds to a halt, because at the word father Miranda's mother starts wailing as if she will never stop. At which Guy and I look at each other in wild surmise, and then we both say surely not.

However, it seems it is, since Miranda's mother meets Trevor Smith years ago, when she is a young married nurse and he is in hospital with his appendix. And once he is released from hospital they do not stop their liaison there, being young & reckless. Indeed they carry on so far that the result is Miranda. But Trevor Smith never knows because after only a couple of weeks of passion he thinks again & absconds, and Miranda's mother is too proud to tell him of his daughter, so instead she raises Miranda as one of the family and otherwise keeps mum.

Guy and I are naturally surprised by this development, though possibly not as much as Miranda & Trevor Smith are about to be, and we are wondering who will inform them of this interesting turn of events when Miranda's mother shoots this line of thought down in mid-flight by saying that she has already done it.

*   *   *

Apparently she sits her daughter down and tells her the instant she enters the house, but Miranda is not disposed to sit or listen, indeed she accuses her loving mother of many unpleasant motives including jealousy & wishing to spoil her life and so on, and demands to see the birth certificate as proof, which of course Miranda's mother cannot supply, and by the end of the conversation Miranda is not speaking to her mother beyond insults.

Following which Miranda's mother sets her sights on Trevor Smith, and at the mention of his name she stops wailing altogether, and quite a scary expression comes over her face. Since it seems that she casts aside her pride and steadies her nerves and gives Trevor Smith the lowdown while he is trying to phone for a taxi, and after she finishes, Trevor Smith laughs merrily and replies oh really? and tells her that if he had a fiver for every female who'd tried that on him over the years he would be in a villa in Monte Carlo by now instead of a little flat in Clapham, so if it is maintenance she is after she can forget it.

While she is relating this Miranda's mother is starting to look quite strange, and does not even respond when Guy and I say we think we had better leave now. So we slip quietly out, and on the way we pass the little room where by the sounds of it Trevor Smith is now out & snoring. Guy wishes to kick his head in, but in the end we feel that this would disturb Miranda's mother even more than already, if that were possible, and head home.

But a few days later I am reading the News of the World over breakfast, when I see a small headline on page four saying ROCK STAR IN OVERDOSE HORROR, and it is referring to Trevor Smith. And the news is that Trevor Smith takes far too much of his smack that evening and does not live to regret it, but is discovered stone cold by Miranda's mother the next morning. A syringe is found by his body, his fingerprints all over it, and the police are saying he must have injected himself sometime in the middle of the night and tried to crawl for help, but never made it. And the News of the World adds a few paras on how wild Trevor Smith is formerly, and how many women he enjoys the benefit of in his lifetime and so on, as the News of the World tends to in such cases.

But I am quite thoughtful for a while, since I am wondering about the version of events the police have constructed. I can see a different scenario in my head, which is Miranda's mother getting up after Guy and I drive away and going downstairs to find Trevor Smith snoring with his bag of smack next to him; and I do not choose to think about what might have happened next, though I allow myself to suppose it not unlikely that an ex-nurse will keep a few syringes around the house and will know all a person needs to know about injections and so on.

But of course this is all imagination and wild conjecture, so I calm my mind with the thought that at least Miranda will not be pursuing the Trevor Smith experience; and somehow, whatever happens, I do not believe Miranda's mother will ever tell her.

So I close the paper and forget the talk I had with Trevor Smith that night, in particular the part where he confides that he always chases the dragon, and never uses needles because he is terrified of them, and will not let them near him ever since an appendix operation he had years before.

F I V E

There is much interest & excitement in the civic because the Aylesbury Flasher is dead, and according to the Bucks Free Press all he leaves in explanation is a note saying alas I was too old, which he writes shortly before setting himself swinging. So the community are scanning the front page and swapping memories, and not all of them are complimentary, since the Aylesbury Flasher is not alone in thinking himself past it; in fact opinion is that any flasher who takes five minutes to unbutton should stick to flashing his bus pass. Still, the girls are waxing nostalgic and saying that the canal path will not be the same, and the men are sympathising, as the Aylesbury Flasher is not too discerning about his audience; indeed, it seems to be his final straw when the labrador belonging to an old granny he has been flashing at for months turns out to be a guide dog.

But I am taking only a distant interest in all this, being

almost the only person I know not to have had the pleasure. Besides, I am distracted by business, since Anna the mediterranean manageress's brother is two weeks behind on deliveries, and currently I am reduced to supplying my private stock instead. Which is a cause of consternation all round, the private stock being some-what superior to the public, as many of the community are finding to their surprise before jumping round or falling over or whatever, depending on their drug of choice at the time. And quite a few are starting to mutter about the quality of the old stuff, though as Guy points out during an emergency meeting yesterday, they never complained when they had it.

So I depart for Anna's caff, only to find the shutters down and the door bolted and a note saying the owner is away until whenever, with not so much as an apology for the inconvenience. Then I remember Anna mentioning a visit to Doris in London and am instantly concerned & suspicious, the chances being that Anna will be so dazzled by the bright lights that she will never return.

So I am at a loose end, and am not even likely to run across Guy, who is taking his capri for an emerg-ency service after running across a mutual acquaintance known as Damage, in this case at 60 mph while Damage is driving on the right and consequently wrong side of a blind corner. Guy says his only consolation is that while his capri is a foot shorter, Damage's shiny new golf is no longer, also he is looking forward to thrashing out the matter with Damage in some depth, as soon as Damage is released from Stoke Mandeville.

Eventually I head for the Bell, where Guy & I recently hold business meetings because no one goes there at lunchtimes apart from jehovah's witnesses, who will go anywhere to get rid of the watchtower. And I do not blame them, also it is quite amusing to see them trying. So I am soon settling on to a bar stool ready to sink a pint or two, and I find myself getting the undivided attention of a skinny & melancholy-looking person who is the new landlord, there being no one else for him to focus on. In fact I doubt he can focus at all, as he is leaning on the bar in a way which suggests he would otherwise be taking a close look at the floorboards, and meanwhile downing whisky at a more than medicinal rate.

After a bit he raises his head from where it is hanging at about counter level and says, 'Families,' sounding more like he is thinking of ending one than starting one. And being only a sip down my guinness I cannot beat a retreat, but instead am forced to shrug, which he seems to take as encouragement. He bends down, and after an interval during which it seems unlikely he will come up again, pulls something out from under the counter and shoves it in my direction, saying, 'What do you make of that?'

I find I am looking at an old bit of material which on closer inspection seems to be some kind of home-made mask. It has carefully stitched slits for eyes and a smile-shaped gap for a mouth, and a drawstring at the bottom where a neck would go. Now thanks to the Bucks Free Press I recognise it as the missing mask of the Aylesbury Flasher; and the police are searching high & low for the device with which the Aylesbury Flasher would simultaneously disguise his identity and attempt to strike fear into his victims, though what with one thing & another, and the material being pink & flowery, it never quite had the effect he intended.

Naturally I am wondering what it is doing behind the counter of the Bell, and the landlord's emotional statement that it is an albatross round his neck does not leave me any wiser, but he is in a communicative mood, and is pouring me pints with a lavish if unsteady hand, saying, 'I have to talk to someone,' and not taking er for an answer; and after gulping many more shots of best malt he is opening up like a flower, though one which will probably regret it in the morning.

It seems I am looking at the Aylesbury Flasher's son & heir, or so the landlord informs me, not that he is ever before boasting of this ancestry. In fact, until today he has been as ignorant as the next man, being raised in what he claims is the most normal of homes, with the smell of pasta in the air and his dear departed mother humming O Sole Mio or La dolce Vita as she goes about her cooking, since his family is of italian descent. At which he whips out a well-worn photo, and indeed his dear departed mother is built like a mafia bodyguard with an expression and little moustache to match. But I do not pass comment on this, since Alberto, which is the landlord's name, is gazing at the picture with tears in his eyes crooning she was so beautiful, there being of course no accounting for taste.

Now Alberto has always lived at his parents' country cottage in the above manner, and is apparently not regretting a minute of it. On the contrary, on learning he is expected to inhabit the little flat the brewery provides over the Bell he is mortified, but his dear departed mother insists on him taking the plunge regardless, and even packs his bags for him, accompanied by many brave smiles. Thus I gather she is not departed at the time, though seemingly she is working on it, since as soon as Alberto is out of the door she sinks into a decline and is regularly informing him over the wires that she is not expected to last beyond the weekend, although which weekend she does not specify.

Until finally the fatal day arrives, taking everyone by surprise, including the patient, although before then many touching deathbed scenes occur in compensation. In one, his mother takes time out to make Alberto swear on her grave to respect his old dad and carry out all his wishes like a dutiful son, which Alberto does with no qualms at all, since as far as he knows his dad's wishes extend to a couple of shots of grappa of an evening and the odd game of boules, weather permitting.

Once his mother is laid to rest, Alberto keeps the Bell open and tries to get on with his life, according to her instructions, So this morning he is reading the Bucks Free Press in his little flat over the pub & tutting over the sad end of the Aylesbury Flasher, who the police have not yet named, when there is the quack of his novelty doorbell. It is the postman, who hands him a brown paper package which he is delighted to sign for, it being his fortieth birthday.

Before opening the package Alberto dutifully rings his old dad, who he is intending to treat to a slap-up lunch, having noticed him appearing more than usually miserable of late. But he is surprised to find there is no reply, which in view of events is not surprising at all, since his dad is currently lying in a more miserable way than ever on a slab. Alberto, of course does not know this, so he opens the parcel bravely humming happy birthday to me, even though he is really wishing his mother could be there to sing it to him. Or failing that, Alberto adds, a wife or similar, though this is only a passing thought, since it seems no matter how hard he tries he is never finding a candidate he feels is qualified, or indeed vice versa.

'And I may say,' he says now, 'this is a great trial & disappointment to me all my life, since I am not really cut out for spending it in solitary. But even my dear departed mother is not finding a solution, and it is always her fondest wish to see me settled with bambinos and so on.' And here he looks soulfully at a queen-size portrait which is surveying the scene from its pride of place over the bar, and which possibly accounts for the Bell's sudden drop in trade, since it is bearing a strong resemblance to Kitchener, and is fixing even pepsi drinkers with a stern & condemnatory gaze.

But anyway, Alberto continues, it is probably a blessing he is not in the company of the fairer sex, because within seconds of opening the package he is reeling back in horror and using most undomestic language. The package contains not only the Aylesbury Flasher's mask, but sixteen pages of his old dad's handwriting explaining the works, and by the time Alberto gets through it he also gets through a bottle of brandy and approximately six thousand cigs, so the last thing he needs is a PS.

But there is a PS, and relating it to me Alberto has a funny turn and hits the bottle again. Because the PS informs him that his old dad's dying wish is for Alberto to take over as the Aylesbury Flasher, being under the impression that Alberto will make a better flasher than he ever was and will expunge the shame of his frequent failures, not to mention the blot on the family's honour and other such exotic & foreign concepts in between.

While Alberto is choking over this and wondering if he can pretend he never saw it, he notices a PPS which says remember your sacred promise to your mother, see enclosed. At which an old get-well-soon card drops out of the envelope, and Alberto recognises it with a sinking feeling as one he sends his mother. Inside, there is a little verse saying mum you are the tops, the best there is in town, no matter what or when or how, I'll never let you down, which even at the time Alberto does not think much of on a poetic level, but is the only one the corner shop has in stock.

So though Alberto is still trying to drown his sorrows he finds they are practically cross-channel standard. Not only is he suddenly an orphan on his birthday, he is also more than a little preoccupied by his unexpected inheritance, and wondering why his dad could not have stayed with exhibiting his garden veg at which he was actually quite successful, winning many commendations for his marrows and so on at county shows.

But from the way Alberto then starts going on about blood ties & italian honour & duty & how he promised his mother and the rest of it, he seems to be coming round to the idea, and after a few more draughts he is mumbling I suppose I should get out more, it is not healthy being shut in a pub all day.

With these words he collapses on top of a peanut display, so I ease myself off the stool and head thoughtfully for the door, and if I am thinking anything it is that Aylesbury is hitting an unlucky streak as far as its flashers go. But on top of this I think it is fortunate for Alberto that Anna picks this time to go awol, since she and his dear departed mother look like two peas, apart from not being green and so on, and in my opinion Alberto has already had enough of his dear departed mother to last him a lifetime.

But soon I am regretting this thought, as Anna seems to have taken root in London and I am having to stay home to avoid the begging & pleading of my friends & acquaintances, not to mention the more aggressive attitude of the ones on ajax as a last resort. And after days of soaps and quiz shows I am thinking it is no wonder our best spliff customers turn out to be housewives, and that when I get my supply back I will suggest they try something stronger. I am almost contemplating dusting and so on when Guy, who is going through much the same thing on the other side of town, finally snaps and rings Anna at Doris's claiming he is a duty sergeant at the Aylesbury station passing on the news that her caff has just burnt down.

*   *   *

After many cries of grief and horror and a hasty but sat-isfying chat with her insurance company, Anna hotfoots it back home planning what to spend the cash on. And following a decent interval to let her recover from the shock of finding the caff still standing, Guy & I pay her a call during which we also sort a delivery for the following Sunday.

So we pass the word round to general relief & cele-bration, and from Sunday onwards Aylesbury is as quiet as the grave, and the police are puzzling and bar owners are despairing, because their regulars are all at home happily hoovering up powder or whatever takes their fancy.

A few days later I am inside the caff raising Anna's spirits with some light conversation, as ever since her abrupt return she is noticeably moody. Also she is forever saying, 'If I find who pulled that fire stunt I will kill them,' and Guy & I are naturally concerned for her peace of mind, since the thought of her moving to pastures new and leaving us high & dry again is too unpleasant to contemplate.

But Anna does not seem to want her spirits raised; in fact she continues to serve her clientele in a silent if not funereal manner. So I am examining a copy of the Bucks Free Press that a previous customer has discarded, and soon am reading with more than usual interest, since reports are coming in from all over that the Aylesbury Flasher is alive & well and once more open to the public. This new incarnation is proving considerably more active, and there are many interviews with distressed victims ranging from the mayoress to a busload of WI members exploring the sights of Aylesbury, who seemingly have more success than they bargain for.

It is as near as it ever is to opening time, so I say my farewells to Anna and set off down the High St. And I am shortly tucking into a pint & congratulating Alberto on an impressive set of results, at which he rolls his eyes wildly and says, 'You have not heard the half of it.'

It seems that, many hours after our first encounter, Alberto wakes with his face in a pile of half-chewed peanuts, which he is apparently snacking on in his stupor, and for some time after he takes to his bed, & often thinks about dying but does not feel up to it. While he gets acquainted with his ceiling in this fashion, Alberto has many opportunities to consider his old dad's last request, and is resolutely saying no never. But one morning he rises from his pillow, having a hot date at the crematorium, and while his parent is being kebabbed behind the curtain, Alberto remembers his sacred promises and is hit by catholic guilt, and from Alberto's description catholic guilt is a world-class heavyweight, because he barely lasts a round at a solitary wake in the Bell afterwards.

That afternoon Mad Ethel the bag lady is staggering along the canal side singing I've got a luvverly bunch of coconuts in an enthusiastic but tuneless way as is her wont. When she is stopped in her tracks, since the path in front of her is filled by what seems to be the Aylesbury Flasher, mask and all, and Mad Ethel is flattered & touched by this return from the grave, having nurtured a soft spot for the Aylesbury Flasher when he is alive & kicking.

There follows a short pause, with Ethel somewhat unsure as to the correct etiquette on such occasions, and the spirit appears to be equally unsure, since after some thought it comes out with, 'Ah hah,' and leers in a less than convincing fashion.

To which Ethel replies, 'Ah hah?' This appears to stump it completely, because after hastily doing up its mac it legs it into the foliage.

Ethel shrugs and staggers on her way, and meanwhile Alberto is crouching behind a bush thinking he can hear his old dad's ashes whizzing round in their little pot, since the idea is to expunge the blot on the family honour etc, and currently he feels he is turning it into more of an oil slick. So he lurks & waits, and after a bit he hears the light patter of female footsteps, at which he leaps out shouting ah ha in what is an almost professional manner. And hearing satisfying cries of astonishment coming from the female in front of him Alberto is about to spring away dramatically when he notices that the female is not alone; in fact she is clutching the hand of a small child who is gazing at him with an expression of horror on its innocent features.

Alberto is equally horrified, since corrupting minors is never part of his game plan, and is reminded of his nephews & nieces in Italy who in the past have enjoyed nothing better than a romp with their uncle Alberto. Alberto dreads to think what their fathers would do to someone who romps in this fashion before them, but suspects whatever it is would involve a dose of concrete and a one-way trip down the river, as many of the fathers are dons, though not the Oxford type.

He is standing superglued to the spot with remorse when there is a sudden shriek & a splash, and Alberto sees that the small child has taken advantage of this distraction and has eased out of the female's restraining grasp and into the water. And though it is shouting, 'Look at me,' Alberto is not, having decided to cut his losses and scarper.

But he finds himself rooted to the ground, since the female latches on to his mac like a man-trap saying, 'Oh save my baby, save my baby.'

Alberto asks her with some irritation to desist, as the

child looks quite contented, in fact it is cavorting like a resident life form, not that there are any. But at these words the child begins throwing up its hands in the air and shouting, 'Save me, save me,' and the female is staring at him with accusation written all over her features, and the child is now shouting, 'I'm going under,' and giving off loud gurgling noises, so Alberto takes a reluctant breath and dives in to find the water is five inches deep.

And when he comes round and floats to the surface, both female and child have disappeared into the distance, and Alberto trails miserable & dripping back to the Bell.

Understandably, his first action on reaching his flat is to take the mask out of his pocket & attempt to rend it into pieces, but after a while Alberto is puffing & panting and gazing at the mask with intense dislike, since despite his biceps' best efforts his old dad's stitching is holding firm. And the mask continues to smirk at him in what Alberto feels is an unnecessarily smug manner, until eventually he gives up and thrusts it to the back of his airing cupboard, after which he pointedly slams the door and retires exhausted.

But the first thing Alberto sees on opening his eyes the next morning is the mask, perched jauntily over a bed post, and though it is smiling down at him in greeting

Alberto does not return the compliment; indeed he utters a startled moan and takes instant shelter beneath his pillow. And when he eventually sticks an eye round the pillowcase corner he finds the mask does not evaporate in the meantime, so Alberto tries to think sensibly, and after a time decides he must have fetched the mask in his sleep. Though he has not the faintest why he should wish to do this asleep or otherwise, he nevertheless leaps on this solution with great relief, the alternatives being too unpleasant to contemplate.

However, it seems that catholics are a superstitious race, believing in all manner of items such as ghosts & angels & the devil & god and so on, and though Alberto comes down firmly on the side of reason he continues eyeing the mask from a safe distance. In fact he is hovering & havering and is no nearer deciding what to do with it when the doorbell quacks loudly, and Alberto realises with a start that he has failed to polish his teeth or comb his hair, and is soon running round in small circles saying help.

Because Alberto has a date, courtesy of a friendly local agency, and though by now he is resigned to such dates being fruitless this one is something of a landmark, being the first time his dear departed mother is not available to dispense tea & wisdom & opinions as to dress sense.

*   *   *

As he heads towards the door, Alberto is dismayed to find himself less than distressed by this notion, and is taking himself sternly to task for such selfish sentiments, though as it transpires he could have saved himself the bother. Because the date's first words on entering Alberto's little flat are, 'Who is that?' owing to the fact that in Alberto's sitting room alone are seventeen framed photos of his dear departed mother, and these are not counting the group shots. In fact, she looks like a choice of wallpaper. And Alberto is half-way through explaining when he feels a draught and hears the patter of high heels followed by a final-sounding bang, and turns round to discover the date has departed without even waiting for sherry.

So Alberto says she is obviously a lowlife person with no taste or family feeling to speak of, and he would prefer not to.

But in her haste the date has left her bag discarded on the sofa, and being brought up around handbags Alberto knows their importance, even to a female of this type. So he follows the noise of fading footsteps down the street and is shortly shouting wait and come back! but if anything the footsteps seem to speed up on hearing his cries. Indeed they are soon galloping along at an impressive pace, and heading off down alleys and doubling back through side streets, and soon Alberto is puffing along after them without the breath to shout anything.

Finally the footsteps lose him by dodging across an intersection, and while Alberto is waiting for the green light and holding his sides and wheezing to himself in some discomfort, he sees a figure which makes him forget about breathing altogether.

Because silhouetted against the traffic cones on the other side of the intersection is what Alberto immediately recognises as the outline of his dear departed mother. As he gazes on this apparition with some astonishment, it seems to beckon to him, though possibly it is just adjusting its headgear, but anyway Alberto does not pause to question, being a little overwhelmed by joy and so on, and the next thing he knows he is waking with his head pillowed on the tarmac, having forgotten everything he ever learnt about the green cross code in his excitement.

Fortunately he is only mildly dented, which is something of a miracle, since in front of him is a scene similar to carnage, with upended lorries & two-storey cars and many drivers wandering round like dazed zombies. But once he has shaken off a most persistent person who is pointing at the remains of an XJS with a trembling finger saying, 'Twenty years without a scratch & now this,' he sees that his dear departed mother has vanished into thin air without so much as stopping to enquire about her son's health or safety first. And no matter how much Alberto searches and pleads and calls out mama she does not return, which Alberto feels is pretty poor behaviour, for an apparition or otherwise.

So he limps somewhat sulkily home, and the first thing he sees is the mask smiling at him from the bed post in what seems to be a sympathetic fashion. And shortly afterwards a mac-clad shape flits from the back door of the Bell, and Alberto is presently prowling the highways & byways of Aylesbury with a spark in his eye and a spring in his stride, in which mood he encounters the WI and the mayoress and so on.

To his surprise, Alberto discovers quite a taste for his inheritance once he puts his back into it, and whenever he finds himself at a loose end is out & about surprising and entertaining the population instead. He tells me modestly it is really only a hobby, though he feels he is gaining in confidence nightly, since the pouncing & prowling & night air are improving his fitness and straightening his posture and putting roses in his cheeks and so on. In fact he is noticing many appreciative glances from the new area crisp and snack representative, an attractive person going under the name of Miss Camilla Miller. But, Alberto says, Miss Camilla Miller & her glances will have to wait, since he does not have a spare moment to pursue them. And here Alberto sighs and tries to look regretful, but fails.

*　　　*　　　*

Before I drain my guinness & leave, Alberto mentions that he has replaced his dear departed mother's portrait over the bar with something more classic, and indeed I see there is now a bleeding deer losing a fight to many jack russells or similar. Alberto explains that his customers seem to prefer it.

S I X

Early one morning, just as the sun is rising, I find myself in the centre of Chearsley with my head resting against a convenient lamppost & feeling less than on top of things thanks to an all-night event somewhere in the neighbourhood. Somehow I make it to the bus stop, the only other option being a lift back with Damage, and though Damage claims to have found a new and exciting short-cut, I do not have a wish to cut things that short & say so.

So instead I settle safely on a bench and am getting round to trying out a cig or two when I notice that Chearsley is coming to life, or at any rate there is something moving in the distance. As it gets closer it proves to be my old acquaintance menopausal Simon, who is wearing a drained & haunted look and greets me by saying cigarette in hoarse tones before vanishing behind the bus shelter.

*   *   *

Now last night menopausal Simon claims to be on top form, and is expressing his high spirits by approaching every female present in a suggestive though unsuccessful manner. As a result, the atmosphere is very jolly with many people laughing, since although menopausal Simon is always declaring himself a man of the world, in terms of experience he is less than hardly. And about half-way through the evening, he seems to tire of being the life & soul in this fashion and exits, presumably for Aylesbury and home. It is therefore unexpected to find him still out & about in Chearsley, and I am wondering what he occupies himself with in the meantime, although not for long, since it is in danger of interrupting my thoughts about business. Now that Anna has shaken off her blues and is delivering the goods again, everything is going what you might call great guns or possibly even a whole battalion. So I am passing my time in pleasant contemplation and wondering if the number 10 is likely to put in one of its surprise appearances, when I suddenly recall that menopausal Simon had arrived at the all-night event on his trusty moped.

But when questioned the bus shelter remains silent, so I conclude that menopausal Simon is asleep, or alternatively unconscious. However, he turns out to be alive if not well, and is huddled into some foliage giving out small groaning noises. I prop myself against a corner of the bus shelter and wait, eventually enquiring if there is a problem. Menopausal Simon does not at first reply, and continues toying anxiously with the surrounding greenery, until finally he says with a casual air, 'You know village bike Sandra?'

At which point many things become clear, since in a small way village bike Sandra is something of a legend, having acquired her name for obvious reasons i.e. being Chearsley's top attraction & leisure pursuit. And though never listed in any brochure it is common knowledge that Sandra's opening hours are from nine a.m. sharp until whenever, during which time she can be found trawling the green in search of company or holding court with Chearsley's finest by this very bus stop.

And as a result, village bike Sandra is enjoying widespread popularity in the neighbourhood, though she never looks as though she relishes it, having a sullen & vacant expression which personally I consider not at all enticing. Indeed it seems this is the expression village bike Sandra is born with, and by all accounts it is seen to change only once, and that is back in the days when village bike Sandra is still going to school. Which she has not done for some time, ever since she sets fire to the school hall while inside everyone is singing 'Nearer My God to Thee' in an unintentionally poignant manner.

On hearing she will henceforth be educated at home, village bike Sandra is apparently seen to smile. And shortly afterwards she is entering the full-time role of village entertainer, after which the rest, as they say, is history.

Although it seems from what menopausal Simon is saying that it is actually current events, or at least as current as last night, which is when menopausal Simon is persuaded to down an e for what he confesses is the first time ever. Consequently, after half an hour or so he is being swamped with all kinds of interesting urges, and is more than usually distressed to find none of the girls present feel like sharing them with him, even the ones he asks twice. After a time he is feeling a little desperate, when he is suddenly struck by the thought that he is only minutes away from the centre of Chearsley, where, as menopausal Simon knows from word of mouth, he can more or less count on coming across village bike Sandra.

So menopausal Simon slips out and is delighted to find Sandra at a loose end in the bus shelter, and once introductions are completed they make for an old brown morris marina, which is rusting away on bricks in a side road next to Sandra's family's council gaff, and is regularly used for purposes not mentioned in the owner's manual. And thanks to the e, menopausal Simon is shortly imagining that village bike Sandra is the most beautiful thing he ever lays eyes on; and though the item in question is staring in a non-committal manner at the marina roof, he himself is feeling in seventh heaven and on cloud nine and so on, at least to start with.

But about fifteen minutes later, so menopausal Simon claims, he is reaching the end of his build-up and about to move into the home straight when he hears the disconcerting sound of a car door opening and feels cold air drifting in a passion-killing way around his more sensitive regions, followed by a harsh voice saying, 'Get out of there, you monster.'

Menopausal Simon not unnaturally freezes in surprise, and for an unpleasant moment has visions of having to have village bike Sandra surgically removed, but then a hand on his collar pulls him backwards, and to his relief he discovers he comes off quite easily. But as he finds himself on the pavement looking up at Sandra's dad and Sandra's mum and what appears to be a footy squad of Sandra's big brothers, he begins to realise his problems are far from over. Sandra's mum is shrieking & carrying on and going oh gawd my little girl, what have you done to her, which menopausal Simon reckons should be fairly obvious under the circs. And Sandra's brothers are circling like a flock of famished vultures, while Sandra's dad is toying gently with a baseball bat and saying, 'What do you think my daughter is, eh? You will regret trifling with her honour and no mistake my son.'

*   *   *

Menopausal Simon is about to point out that Sandra's honour is well & truly trifled with before he comes on the scene, but a closer look at the baseball bat dissuades him. Instead he admits truthfully that he is regretting it more than a bit already, at which all the brothers look at each other going not enough and start to move in smacking their lips in a worrying manner.

But while menopausal Simon is trying to sink into the pavement, saying pleadingly, 'Let's be grown up about this,' Sandra's dad says, 'Hold it, hold it,' and raises a hand, at which the brothers obediently hover in their tracks.

Sandra's dad bends over menopausal Simon saying that, even if he was prepared to let bygones be bygones and forgive & forget and so on, since menopausal Simon looks to be truly sorry, at which menopausal Simon nods furiously, there is still one little problem. Menopausal Simon says nervously, 'What is that exactly?' and Sandra's dad says, 'The girl is only fourteen. Look at her, the innocent mite,' and points to Sandra, who menopausal Simon now sees is standing gazing blankly at her feet. Sandra's dad explains that, even letting bygones be bygones etc, it is his duty to call the police, as menopausal Simon has committed a serious offence. At this point he looks very solemn & pious and adds that there is no shortage of witnesses either.

*   *   *

Menopausal Simon grasps the fact that he is caught between a rock and a hard place, and comes to the conclusion that, if his own places are ever hard again, which is seeming unlikely, he will know to stay home with a copy of Big & Bouncy, that being the option he has scorned this very evening. So he moans, 'What am I going to do?' not expecting an answer, and is quite taken aback when Sandra's dad replies, 'How much have you got on you?'

When it becomes clear that Sandra's dad is referring to money, menopausal Simon is struck dumb with surprise and hands over his wallet without a murmur. And so he finds himself making a contribution to the family's living expenses, which leaves him cleaned out for a month, but Sandra's dad mentions that it could be worse, and as he is still holding the baseball bat menopausal Simon is not inclined to argue.

So finally menopausal Simon is allowed to get up from the pavement, which he does with what dignity he can muster i.e. not much. And as he sets off down the road to cries of come again soon followed by much sniggering, he discovers he is feeling more than a little sorry for Sandra, who seems to be the only one of her family not enjoying the whole affair.

I am not surprised by this, as menopausal Simon is known for being a soft touch when it comes down to it and has just about given up trying to pretend otherwise. But he insists he is feeling more sorry for himself, expecially when he remembers his trusty moped is parked outside Sandra's house, and even he is not soft enough to risk collecting it. He therefore seeks refuge in the village phone box, and is going through his pockets to see if Sandra's dad has missed a ten-pence piece with which to call home, when he hears a muffled cough and looks round to see village bike Sandra standing outside.

With recent events in mind, menopausal Simon is not pleased by this discovery, and checks the coast in case any of her family have tagged along, but it seems to be clear, so he relaxes a little. But to be on the safe side he keeps his nose pointed firmly into the receiver, and as he is getting only an echoing silence from the other end he begins nervously humming a little tune to pass the time. But he stops, on hearing village bike Sandra's voice announcing from outside, 'That is lovely,' and when menopausal Simon finally turns, he sees that she has a strange look in her eye, and is pressed up against the glass like a lovestruck spaniel.

In a flash, menopausal Simon remembers the many things he has said to village bike Sandra while in the throes of passion & e, and though warning bells are clanging he finds himself opening the door and saying, 'Do you really think so?' since the little tune he is humming is one of his own composition.

It seems that village bike Sandra does think so, and moreover she cannot believe that menopausal Simon has written it all by himself, and while a voice inside menopausal Simon's head is still urging him to run for it, aloud he is saying, 'Oh that is nothing, wait until you hear this.'

And so for some time menopausal Simon entertains village bike Sandra with his ditties; and having never had an audience before he is more than a little flattered by her response, which is of the hand-clasping and starry-eyed variety. But every time he pauses for breath village bike Sandra edges closer with her bosom heaving, and pretty soon menopausal Simon is gasping for air and casting frantically round for inspiration. He is la-la-la-ing away with fading vigour when he hears village bike Sandra saying sharply, 'I know that one,' since he is now working his way though the top forty, and before he can hit another note he is pinned to the back of the phone box and rendered helpless in a lip-lock.

When village bike Sandra finally disengages, menopausal Simon is gazing at her with some enthusiasm, since this time village bike Sandra seems to be giving it her all, and her all is not to be sneezed at. And in no time at all the phone box is rolling & heaving & bulging at the seams, and menopausal Simon is crying yipee with anticipation. But soon he is crying, 'What?'

because something seems to be missing, and menopausal Simon notices this almost immediately on account of the something being village bike Sandra.

When he surfaces, menopausal Simon's gaze is met by a solid person in a pointy blue hat and bicycle clips, with a truncheon dangling from one hand and village bike Sandra dangling from the other. 'Now then, now then,' says this person, or something along those lines, 'what are we playing at?' and for a second menopausal Simon is tempted to reply poker, but does not, having an unhealthy respect for the law. Since the solid person is the Chearsley village constable, who is frequently seen cycling round the lanes in an impressive & crime-deterring manner, and menopausal Simon is easily impressed & deterred, especially when caught red-handed with a minor. So he is holding out his wrists for the bracelets, only to find the constable is turning to village bike Sandra and saying, 'Does your father know you're out?' And when Sandra replies in the negative, the constable says, 'Least said soonest mended,' and with this cryptic comment cycles off into the distance.

Menopausal Simon is not unnaturally surprised by this lax approach and turns to village bike Sandra with a fistful of questions. At first she is eyeing him somewhat suspiciously, but he persists in a gentle and non-threatening manner, and eventually village bike Sandra is sitting trustingly beside menopausal Simon in the phone box and eating out of his hand, and also telling him the story.

It seems that Sandra's family take a dim view of her freelancing outside the marina, but they are otherwise supportive & encouraging of her biking. Since over the years many sad saps in the menopausal Simon line have come & gone rather poorer and sadder than when they arrived, and on these occasions Sandra's dad is wont to pat her on the head, saying a few more of them and I can retire, even though he has not worked for years thanks to his dodgy back playing up every time he visits the job centre.

And thanks to Sandra's dad no one ever interferes in her affairs, since he lets it be known in many small but pointed ways that his family is his own affair, one of these small ways being a chisel. Whether it ends up in someone's tyre or garden gnome or rabbit, anyone who tries to interfere gets the point. And after the vicar discovers his prize fishpond is now a patio, someone having placed a sack of cement in it overnight without removing the fish first, Chearsley finally sees the sense of resigning itself to the inevitable, while the village constable, who is long ago at school with village bike Sandra's parent and is therefore respecting his abilities more than most, steers his bicycle well clear & looks firmly in the opposite direction, except when Sandra's dad is favouring him with pints down the local.

On hearing this, menopausal Simon is filled with disquiet & outrage, and he takes village bike Sandra by the hand and says, 'You are too good for this, Sandra.'

Instead of denying this, village bike Sandra stiffens as though in sudden back pain, after which she starts to go watery around the edges, and shortly menopausal Simon's shoulder is in the middle of a full-scale flood, with village bike Sandra saying to it, 'O what am I going to do?' in between sniffs. Because it seems that village bike Sandra is sick of biking and has never enjoyed it in the first place, no matter how much her father insists on the many side benefits, e.g. fresh air & exercise.

After this, village bike Sandra returns to being female in a loud & penetrating fashion, and menopausal Simon finds himself saying, 'There there,' and patting her comfortingly on the shoulder. And soon she is mopping up her cheeks with menopausal Simon's old hankie, and he is opining that something must be done, and moreover informing village bike Sandra that for any money he will go & kick her dad's head in there & then, although by now he is doubtless tucked up in bed and out of range.

At which village bike Sandra lets out a little yelp saying, 'My hero,' and embraces menopausal Simon warmly, and there follows a moving & touching scene which menopausal Simon says he prefers to draw a veil over.

But the upshot is that village bike Sandra leaves for home under the firm impression that menopausal Simon is more than just a passing fancy. In fact they have a date set for tomorrow night. And being knocked for six by this unexpected result, menopausal Simon spends the rest of the night roaming the streets of Chearsley in a happy and somewhat romantic daze.

Only in the cold light of morning is he struck by the potential difficulties of introducing village bike Sandra as his loving partner, on top of which he is old enough to be her social worker. With this thought, menopausal Simon sinks back on the ground saying it must be the e, he would never behave in this fashion other-wise; and I am looking serious & thoughtful & so on, and not telling him that the only e's at the all-night event are nothing but aspirin, since I supply them. Because somehow I do not feel this knowledge will do menopausal Simon any good, and am fairly certain that village bike Sandra will not either. So I reassure him that village bike Sandra is doubtless just having a good laugh at his expense, it being widely known that she is something of a tough cookie and all-purpose man-trap.

Menopausal Simon does not look one bit reassured at this; in fact he goes quite silent for a while, before saying, 'Do you really think so?' And on finding that indeed I do, he does not brighten up any; and when I begin listing Sandra's track record he holds up a hand saying all right all right, I get the picture.

Eventually menopausal Simon sighs & says he can see it will never work, and forsaking his moped & village bike Sandra forever, climbs on to the number 10 and returns to Aylesbury, resigning himself once again to his bachelor lifestyle. But he remains unnaturally quiet and solemn, no matter how much he is taken out and filled with bevvies, and everyone is wondering what is up but is left to wonder in vain. And every so often I remind menopausal Simon that there are other fish to fry, though admittedly, if there are any, they are keeping their distance, and menopausal Simon just sits there gazing into space and saying nothing in what I sense is a somewhat resentful fashion.

A few nights later, the two of us are down the Kings Head passing time in this fashion. And consequently when one of the undercover detectives drifts over I greet him with some relief; also he is not bad for his sort, and is fond of relating stories concerning police work, pretending they come from a mate of his on the force. At first menopausal Simon ignores the conversation, but soon the detective is asking if we hear what occurs in Chearsley this morning, and at the mention of Chearsley menopausal Simon pricks up his ears and sighs, since recently he has not had the heart to go near it.

*   *   *

When we reply in the negative, the detective says that it is a shame, since what is left of Chearsley is buzzing, which has never happened in living memory. And it seems that, on the day after village bike Sandra bids a fond & loving farewell to menopausal Simon, Chearsley's residents wake up to what they all say is a new & different village bike. The first sign is that, come nine a.m., the bus stop is deserted, and many local lads are hanging round it looking something like spare parts. And when village bike Sandra eventually emerges it is only for a brief stroll, and all the residents remark on how her face lacks its usual sullen & vacant expression; indeed, many of the locals are saying she looks like she is on cloud nine, though many are saying it is drugs.

But as the days pass it seems that Sandra's face is slowly sinking downwards. In fact, the statement from the post office, which she visits yesterday morning and where she buys one popsicle and a twelve pack, puts it at about ground level, if not below. So now the residents are commenting on the fact that Sandra is back to normal. Indeed, after many loud & persuasive arguments are accidentally overheard by her next-door neighbours, she emerges yesterday at five to nine and proceeds to spend the day in a healthy, outdoor fashion.

When it gets dark she is still wandering up and down the green keeping a lookout for company, but by now Chearsley is like a desert apart from the absence of sand and camels and so on and the fact that it is chucking it down. Because of the cold and generally cheerless weather, even Sandra's most reliable admirers are nowhere in sight, though it seems that Sandra can see the bright lights of the Chearsley Bell across the road, and can hear the sounds of merry-making and laughter and shouts of sod it make that a treble, and it is obvious that a good time is being had by all, except possibly the barstaff.

But when Sandra puts her head around the saloon door she is greeted with cries of not tonight, darlin' and advised to go home by all & sundry, which she informs them she cannot do, since her parents have told her she comes back early at her peril. So she loiters for a bit, until the barman shakes his tea towel at her, saying, 'Go on, clear off.' And as Sandra turns away he points to the food counter, which is displaying a range of pub savouries and wilting apple turnovers & assorted pastries, and adds, 'We've got enough little tarts in here already,' at which all his clientele laugh loudly before sticking their faces back in their bevvies.

This is the last the pub's inmates see of village bike Sandra, but some time later the village constable spots her walking towards her front door in what he describes as a decisive fashion. What seems to happen next is, when village bike Sandra gets home, by which time her parents are snoring & dead to the world, she does not go to bed but heads straight for the kitchen, where she turns the gas up to full and apparently forgets to light it.

Though the detective tells us that, in his view, this is a deliberate act of destruction, since many things are emerging about village bike Sandra's family and not any of them are pleasant. In fact from what the detective hears he would willingly buy village bike Sandra a bevvy, or several, though sadly he has missed his chance. Because Sandra's dad always wakes at around nine o'clock, after which he is in the habit of lighting up his first cig of the morning, and thanks to village bike Sandra, he will never have to worry about the harmful effects of this habit again. In fact they are still sorting out the debris, and chances are, the detective relates, they will be saying the ashes to ashes over assorted items of household furniture, the explosion having been an impressive one.

But this is not all, the detective continues. Earlier that morning, the village constable is pedalling slowly along, his mind elsewhere, when a little moped comes out of nowhere at the speed of a formula one, and proceeds to run him off the road. And although the village constable is not noticing much, being in a ditch & swallowing bits of hedgerow, from behind the figure looks much like that of village bike Sandra.

But if it is village bike Sandra the village constable

is much hurt & puzzled, because before it disappears down the road the figure makes a somewhat offensive gesture in his direction, and he cannot understand why this would be, since he is always priding himself on his community relations.

After telling us this the detective seems to notice he has lost his audience and eventually drifts off, and menopausal Simon and I sit at the bar for a bit saying nothing except same again. Somehow I am feeling that the bevvies should be on me, and menopausal Simon does not dispute this. So we have many more, followed by a game of arrows, and then some extra bevvies, and a few more reckless games of arrows, at which customers start complaining on account of darts landing in their pints etc, and by the end of the evening we have downed enough to take us up to the Kings Head record and are sailing confidently past it. And the last bevvy before we are removed is a toast to village bike Sandra wishing her luck and so on, wherever she is, and this is the only one menopausal Simon insists on buying.

S E V E N

Now Bernie is under the impression that he is being haunted, and by none other than his old friend & bosom companion Clive, which is surprising, particularly as everyone else is under the impression that Clive is not so much dead as merely departed. So when Bernie chooses to confide this news in me one evening, I raise an eyebrow and suggest there is a fact or several that Bernie may wish to add to his statement, and after much thought and many anxious pleas for secrecy Bernie does so.

It seems that Clive's hasty exit from Aylesbury life is not entirely voluntary, and all the time he is apparently residing at a remand centre twenty miles away. It is, Bernie naturally insists, a stitch-up and Clive did not do it, but by the sound of it whatever he did not do is still looking likely to result in Clive doing many years with no remission.

*　　*　　*

At first Bernie is made tearful & distraught by Clive's absence and is resigning himself to a sad and lonely existence, but as the days pass he is actually finding it less sad than when Clive is at large & available, Clive being the loud & opinionated sort who the community prefer to leave to his own devices, these being not at all agreeable. And so gradually Bernie is perking up, and though of course he is still missing Clive like a brother, he is presently feeling this is all relative. And soon he is putting on a braver face altogether and consoling himself with thoughts of the welcome party he will throw for Clive when he is finally released, since Bernie is still convinced that Clive is driven snow, and placing much faith in the justice system, and possibly believing in fairies also, though he does not confirm this.

But Clive obviously does not share Bernie's optimism. Indeed, after being banged up and banged by the more sociable inmates, it seems that Clive has had it up to here in all respects, and one morning Bernie finds a former remand centre inhabitant on his doorstep & delivering a note in Clive's own handwriting. And after Bernie tears it open his heart plummets and his stomach also, and he is saying help, help, although there is none available.

Because just before Clive is hauled away in chains he gives Bernie a sum of cash to look after, which he explains is his safety net & pension fund. And the note requests Bernie to use as much as is needed to hire a getaway driver, who should be outside the remand centre at midnight the following Monday, by which time everyone inside will be tucked up in bed & snoring, and Clive will be able to make good his escape.

The only problem with this is that by now it is already noon on Monday, and Bernie finds himself in something of a situation, having not a clue how to acquire a getaway driver at such short notice, other than frequenting banks etc in the hope that one will come along. He is therefore casting frantically around for inspiration when he runs across Damage in the Bugle Horn, and Bernie never has the privilege of driving with Damage, and is somehow of the opinion that he gets his name for being a hard customer. So in desperation he offers Damage the job for a tenner, and to Bernie's delight Damage reckons it will be a laugh & accepts.

Bernie returns chirpily home, thinking all his problems are sorted; and it is only later on, when he & Damage are accelerating towards the remand centre, that he begins to feel the first flutters of doubt. Since it is immediately obvious that Damage is speeding in both senses, and after he repeatedly overtakes on the inside when there is no inside to speak of, and goes over a roundabout, literally, and turns many cats into flat ones, Bernie's flutters are more of a violent banging; in fact he is beginning to suspect he is having a cardiac.

To start with, Bernie tries to protest at this unprofessional behaviour, but by the time they are approaching the remand centre he is both rigid and speechless, so when they see a small, dark figure climbing over the wall, it is Damage who remarks, 'Look, he's early,' of which there is no doubt, as they have done the trip in what Bernie reckons is world-record time, though oddly it seems to have gone on for centuries.

On seeing Clive hitting the ground in the distance Damage hits the acceleration pedal, and Bernie is flung back in his seat as the car shoots forward, and tries to shut his eyes, but cannot because of the g forces. So he sees all of what happens next in a kind of slo-mo; one minute Clive is running towards them with a liberated expression on his features, and the next he is slowing down and staring at the scene in disbelief. Because it seems that Damage has failed to notice a tree which is loitering somewhere between Clive and his rescuers, and as a result the car bounces gracefully off it, spins through 360 and comes down in what would be a perfect landing were it not upside-down.

Meanwhile Bernie is seeing the world go round and round and not enjoying it, and then he is suddenly seeing it from the wrong way up and not liking that much either, but what his attention is mainly fixed on is a hub cap. It is previously a fairly innocuous hub cap, actually Bernie does not remember noticing it before, but he is noticing it now since it is hurtling away from the crash site and towards Clive like a guided missile.

The last Bernie sees of Clive's face before the hub cap hits him is a look of utter disgust, after which Clive collapses like a broken doll and lies still, and Bernie has just time to notice that Clive's neck is resembling a U-bend before Damage suggests they should be leaving, as there are doubtless officials and so on who will be taking an interest in proceedings. And finding Bernie unresponsive, Damage slaps some sense into him in quite a forceful fashion.

When Bernie comes round the world is still at the wrong angle, and for some time he believes he is still in the car, though it transpires he is being carried along a small side road by a panting & somewhat resentful Damage. But presently he is the right way up again and saying back back back since his vocabulary seems to have temporarily deserted him.

Indeed Damage is to later admit he cannot credit his hearing, since Bernie appears to be suggesting that they return to Clive's rescue; and when Damage disagrees profoundly with this idea Bernie sobs and moans and starts looking as though he is about to stagger back under his own steam. Eyeing Bernie up, Damage comes to the conclusion it is not safe to allow him his head, since Bernie is not the sort to hold out under interrogation.

In fact Damage is reckoning that if Bernie returns to the remand centre he might as well turn himself in and save Bernie the bother.

So Damage tells Bernie that there is no point, Clive is dead, which in Damage's book he quite probably is. At this news Bernie pauses and goggles and says what? To which Damage replies as a dodo, and that he checks Clive's pulse before they leave, though of course Bernie will not remember this, being unconscious at the time.

Here Bernie lets out a little whimper and his eyes roll round like snooker balls, after which Damage sees him collapse less than elegantly to the ground where he remains with his toes turned up. So Damage slings him over his back in the manner of a fireman, and after many long miles he is finally staggering into town when Bernie's eyelids flutter and he mutters in a faint voice, dead, dead, and Damage says yes, yes, and suggests that he will now be off home. But once he puts Bernie down & straightens him out, Bernie's first tottering steps appear to be leading him directly to the local police station; and when Damage asks what he thinks he is playing at, Bernie replies somewhat confusedly that he has to find news of Clive, as perhaps Damage is mistaken.

Now Damage has to think rapidly & act more so, and the next time Bernie comes round he is lying in his own bed with Damage leaning over him solicitously and saying he must be concussed, which by now he doubtless is. And when Bernie tries to move he finds his legs will not let him, as Damage appears to be sitting on them. After some discussion Bernie is out of denial & facing up to the fact that Clive has been cut short and down in his prime, and though he then seems to go into shock and is lying motionless under his pillow, Damage still does not trust him a centimetre. So he determines to stay at least until the morning, by which time Bernie will hopefully have grown out of any foolish inclinations to confide in the forces of law & order.

It is a dark & stormy night, and outside Bernie's two up the trees are tossing and the wind is wuthering and the occasional owl is getting to make itself heard over all of the above, when suddenly Bernie sits bolt upright in bed and says, 'Listen.' Since from outside is coming a strange moaning & murmuring, and on closer hearing it is heard to say, 'Bernie, Bernie.'

In a flash Damage realises that Clive must have beaten the odds after all, and he sees trouble ahead, and many explanations, and also has little desire to encounter Clive at the best of times, which this is not. So when Bernie says, can you hear it? Damage replies no. He is preparing to maintain this line for as long as it takes when Bernie lets out a great wail and hides under his duvet, and by the morning he seems firmly convinced

the voice is a visitation, which is how Damage is happy
to leave it.

Bernie spends the next few days recovering in bed, and
as a result is missing the following press coverage if
there is any. But anyway, he tells me, the voice seems
to be a one-off, because although he is spending many
sleepless nights it does not return. But his conscience
is ever present, and turning his food into ashes in his
mouth, and worse still his bevvies too.

By this stage no one has spoken to Damage, who has disappeared for a motoring holiday in Scotland, and I can
think of no way of consoling Bernie, apart from suggesting that he tries something new, such as campari, and on
hearing this Bernie exits in some distress saying that no
one ever takes him seriously, which it is true they do not.

So I head off to meet up with Guy, since we are having
to do some business with the local squat. And for
once I am reluctant, since calling round at the squat
is generally a depressing affair, thanks to the place
being breezeblocked like a fortress and the presence of
unpleasant types like security men and council officials
lurking & trying to find a breach in the squatters'
defences. On top of this the squatters themselves are
not exactly the most cheery bunch; in fact recently it is
as much as anything can do to bring a smile to their lips,
and then only briefly.

There was a time when anyone wanting a squatter used to head for the civic centre of a Saturday, where they could regularly be found busking & strumming guitars & looking hopeful down by the civic steps. It was never the most productive place to busk, the civic not being the centre of anything much, so that the squatters barely made an honest living out of stray shoppers passing by, generally on the other side. And even then it is obvious, due to many choruses of help & the streets of london, that the squatters are unhappy about this state of affairs. And gradually their singing is sounding more & more like a funeral backing track, until one morning Eddie the manager is so moved by a plaintive chorus of Love Me Do drifting in through the civic windows that he instructs the squatters to leave. Since he naturally does not wish his customers to be equally moved and maybe sobbing into their filter coffees, or at any rate being moved to leave without paying for them.

So the squatters are reduced to busking even less impressively outside the public toilets, and with no other means of support, since they are against signing on on the grounds that it is immoral. And at a poker game only last night Guy points out that it is lucky the squatters have not yet heard about the bypass or we could be looking at another Jonestown or similar, though obviously on a smaller scale.

Everyone present at the time agrees, knowing about the

bypass from Guy's father who is privy to this kind of info, and who is rubbing his hands with glee at the very thought. Because although the bypass is to be quite small and not really bypassing anything apart from the chippy, it is scheduled to go right through the squat and back again, and Guy's father, like most mature residents, holds no brief for squatters, claiming he will happily tarmac over the place personally, so long as the squatters are in it at the time.

Privately the gathering also believe that the squatters are somewhat slow and backward, otherwise they would be on benefit and in pleasant council accommodation instead, but they are not about to endorse Guy's father whatever, and there is a moment or so of supportive silence before Guy comments, 'My deal,' and things return to normal. Though normal by now is a rather blurred & careless state, since by this stage there is not much left of Guy's home-grown, which is a small sideline he is recently cultivating in his father's old greenhouse. And this home-grown is a very calming experience; in fact it is so calming that the only problem is raising an interest or even an eyelid afterwards.

Thoughtfully Guy has saved the squatters an ounce, saying that their need is probably greater. Which indeed it seems to be, because once we are at the squat & sipping at a communal can of beer and admiring the Home Sweet Home inscribed in felt tip over the mantelpiece, the video expires half-way through Hellraiser, and it is clear the council have finally discovered that the squatters are borrowing their electric supply from the street lights and have disconnected them, not caring if they are left in the dark about the plotline or even generally.

But soon a candle is found to roll by and a guitar is strumming and the squatters' dogs are all whining gently in sympathy, when someone produces a nose flute. Guy is obviously shaken by this development, since in an unguarded moment he mentions the bypass. But the squatters simply respond, 'Oh, that,' and from this lacklustre reaction it seems that no one is intending to protest or march or even chain themselves to bull-dozers, the latter being the logical option as, with only six residents, any marches are likely to get overlooked. In fact there are mutterings about chucking it all in, with many squatters commenting bitterly on how it is hardly worth breaking into these deserted old places any more; indeed, they hardly get time to stand let alone squat before they are out again.

The thing is, confides one of the squatters while he is unlocking & unbolting & unchaining the back door for us, there is currently a problem closer to home than the bypass, and when Guy asks how close he looks at the ceiling and replies, upstairs. But he refuses to go into detail and ushers us through the door saying mind how you go, though too late to stop Guy falling over a somewhat hostile doberman the security men keep releasing into the wilds of the back garden.

Eventually the doberman departs a sadder & wiser animal, and Guy brushes a speck of dust off his sleeve, after which we depart. Although we are soon basking in the warmth & comfort of menopausal Simon's coal-effect fire, our thoughts turn to the squat on more than one occasion, in fact it is twice, with Guy saying the squatters can keep it, in a heartfelt fashion.

Indeed, while we are relaxing & enjoying, it is a different story back at the squat. After we exit the squatters soon discard their guitars and nose flutes and other lame attempts at jollity, and sit instead in silence staring at the ceiling, from whence can be heard the clump of heavy boots. Soon enough they are clumping downstairs, and the sound is followed by the entrance of a short & squat squatter with what looks like a dead sheep on his head but is actually dreadlocks. And the dogs are whimpering and glancing nervously at his boots and many are slinking for cover, and were it not for the effects of Guy's home-grown it is possible the squatters would be following suit. Because, though there is no such thing as a chief squatter, squatters being in favour of brotherhood and equality and so on, this particular squatter is under the impression that there is, and also that it is him, and the other squatters are wishing they were not quite so much in favour of brotherhood & the rest of it, as most would be on for giving him a good kicking.

But no one dares object, since they are more than a bit apprehensive of Barry, this being his name. Also Barry has a sad & melancholy tale, which he insists on telling whenever he is asked to wash up or clean or similar, and by now the squatters are word perfect in the story of how everyone Barry ever lives with, such as his mother, his aunt, his grandparents etc, always tires of his company. Indeed, by the time Barry is evicted from his cousin's he has finally run out of relatives, in which pathetic state he turns up at the squat. And once there he refuses to depart even for a second, saying that every time he leaves anywhere else someone changes the locks behind him.

But it has not taken long for the other squatters' sympathies to swing in a somewhat opposite direction; in fact they are rapidly thinking quite kindly of Barry's nearest & dearest. Because Barry is showing an uncanny knack for saying the wrong thing at the right time, and as a result the squat's formerly friendly and united atmosphere soon changes into something more suited to a footy pitch, with squatter turning against squatter and many rows & sulks & tears in corners, and an air of apathy similar to that of the England squad after a world cup qualifier.

However, this evening, all Barry says is, 'Where will it all end?' before removing a candle and exiting, which does not leave the squatters any happier. And when one squatter pulls out a copy of The DSS & You and begins flicking through it, there are noticeably few catcalls; in fact no one so much as raises an eyebrow, and not only thanks to the homegrown.

But after a while the squatter throws the volume down, saying what is he doing up there, since the clumping upstairs has not stopped but is sounding like Barry is practising a scottish reel. To which there are replies of who cares, though if the squatters could see what was going on, which of course they cannot, it is likely they would care more than usual. Because upstairs Barry is pulling at his dreadlocks and hopping in pain, and with one final tug the dreads spring free revealing the fact that Barry the squatter is Clive himself, and the dreadlocks are nothing but an ill-fitting wig Clive appropriates from the remand centre's alternative production of The Importance of being Ernest. And breathing a sigh of relief, Clive makes for his mattress, but soon he falls again to fretting & cursing & bemoaning his lot, and if Bernie were in the room he would be moaning too, although for different reasons.

Because Clive has a score or many to settle with Bernie, though when he regains consciousness after the hub cap encounter he does not realise this. Naturally enough his only thought then is to leg it, but the closer he gets to town the more Clive is thinking that as soon as Bernie hands over the cash he is for it, since Clive is not taking kindly to being abandoned like a sinking ship & wishes to prove it.

But when he arrives at Bernie's he finds his tactful attempts to get Bernie's attention are greeted with a cold shoulder, and just as Clive is about to heave a brick through the window a patrolling constable wanders past, and Clive is forced to flee for sanctuary. The only place he can think of is the squat, so he dons his wig and the rest is history, though the squatters' charitable welcome sadly fails to move Clive one bit. Indeed, he marks them down as suckers and passes many an amusing hour spreading strife and dissension, there being not much else to pass the time on, at least during daylight hours.

While this is all enjoyable enough, Clive's urgent desire is to get his cash, get Bernie and get out of town, in that order. But he knows he has to wait for any hue and cry to die down, and in the meantime he is grinding his teeth with fury & frustration. Many days pass in this fashion, while outside the squat the bulldozers are being oiled & polished & tuned up in readiness for the bypass. And inside the squat there are now many sarcastic additions to the Home Sweet Home legend over the mantelpiece, the latest being No, this is hell, nor are we out of it, since several of the squatters have a literary bent. Sure enough the day before eviction day the squatters are still not out of it, and although there are many urgent debates about their futures the only thing anyone can agree on is that none of them include Barry, so they are not coming up with anything.

So it seems that, like it or not, the squatters are heading for a final stand, and much of the day is spent practising for the occasion, with squatters gloomily chaining each other to banisters and arranging chairs in front of doors in a half-hearted manner, as they know that, against the sledgehammers and other legal devices, they have not an earthly.

Come early evening it is generally agreed that enough is more than, and without a word to Barry, who is getting in the way of all their efforts and sniggering loudly throughout, the squatters slip off for a final communal bevvy down the Kings Head. It is while they are trying to pay for it with the busking proceeds that Guy & I stop off for take-outs, and finding the squatters still sorting through handfuls of old buttons we invite them back to Bernie's for a farewell smoke, that being our destination.

Within an hour or so everyone is at ease in Bernie's little bedroom, Guy's last bit of home-grown going rapidly up in flames, and the only person not at ease is Bernie, despite the home-grown. Indeed he jumps out of his skin when Damage walks in, having seemingly had enough of Scotland, and for some time seems to be trying to get Damage's private attention. But Damage is ignoring him and leaning negligently on the open window-sill with a spliff he claims for himself on arrival.

Damage is telling Guy how relaxing he is finding it, and Guy is agreeing that it is, and Damage is leaning further & further back in proof, when all of a sudden he is so laid back he is no longer on the window-sill. And from below come the sounds of thudding & thumping, while the rest of the room are left gazing more than a little vacantly at the empty frame and trying to work out what is missing.

After a bit Bernie says, 'Damage,' with an air of discovery, and begins to follow, but before he reaches the bedroom door Damage reappears looking a little out of breath and saying that there is no point in going outside for a while, as it is overrated.

Bernie is staring at him in puzzlement when there is yet another entrance like Clapham Junction, and this time it is menopausal Simon, who staggers in explaining that the door is open, but anyway look what he has found outside. And suddenly everyone is gazing at the comatose figure of Clive on the floor, and their reactions, though slow, are many and varied.

Following this there is much story-swapping with the squatters, and pieces are slowly falling into place, and meanwhile Bernie is sponging a large lump on Clive's brow moaning how could I have left him. But everyone else is celebrating Damage's narrow escape from the crazy paving and agreeing that it is more than a little lucky that Clive is lurking outside for him to land on instead.

Eventually the noise dies down, though when Clive opens his eyes he is greeted by a storm of questions, but to each & every demand it soon emerges that he is simply replying, 'Mmm?' and his eyes have a glazed & blank look, and even when Damage pokes him quite firmly to test his reactions, Clive just responds, 'Mmm?' In fact the only time Clive reacts at all is when Bernie comes back in with a glass of water, and at the sight of him, Clive becomes so agitated that Bernie has to be hastily shown out again, despite his protests.

Much later, the occupants of the room are slumped in silence staring at Clive, who is by now sitting up & looking quite perky, but still not saying anything more interesting no matter who is waving or prodding at him. Although he is waving back, which Damage says is a good sign, and since Damage spends a lot of time around doctors and hospitals etc everyone is relieved to hear it. But no one can think what to do with Clive next, since wherever he goes, including a hospital, he is bound to land up inside again. Indeed, when a hospital is suggested there are loud & emotional sounds of disagreement from the other side of the door, where Bernie is sitting.

In the meantime the squatters are muttering among themselves in a corner. It seems that they are feeling the urge to depart, having finally decided on pastures new, or in this case an abandoned old warehouse in which an acquaintance of theirs in Oxford is currently squatting. And to this end they are not even intending to go back to the Aylesbury squat, having their bags & dogs & so on with them, and reckon the only thing they are missing is the faces of the security men when they arrive in battle formation tomorrow morning.

So they get up to leave and the dogs fall into line behind them, and much to everyone's astonishment so does Clive. The squatters start backing off and saying oh no, and Clive is standing there with a trusting look on his features, and the rest of the room suddenly realises that this is the answer, though the squatters do not like the question at all.

Much later still, the squatters begin to concede that Clive now appears to be relatively harmless, and the rest of the room are saying he is, he is, and Clive himself is contributing, 'Mmmmmm,' in what could well be agreement. But the squatters are still looking dubious.

So, in an inspired moment, Damage suggests that Bernie might like to fund Clive's upkeep on a charitable basis, as sometimes happens with African children and similar. And outside the door Bernie agrees, as long as he can receive regular reports to make him feel better about things. And once he pushes a down-payment under the door, the squatters appear to resign themselves and turn to Clive saying come on then if you have to.

Clive gives the room a final wave and follows them out obediently, though it is noticeable that when he passes Bernie on the stairs he seems to have some kind of seizure. Fortunately it is only a brief one & Bernie is as good as new in a couple of days, having looked more than a bit shop-soiled to start with.

A few weeks later, Bernie is down the Bell waving his first report with much joy & pride, though he is disappointed to find that there is not a photo enclosed, and naturally the community gather round to hear the news with interest. It seems that Clive has settled down well, and moreover he is proving friendly and house-trained and a dab hand with the cleaning, though he is still not saying anything.

But he is showing a remarkable talent for performing, and can apparently be seen every Saturday outside the Randolph Hotel banging a little drum with the rest of the squatters, and looking like he is enjoying himself thoroughly. Indeed the squatters are grooming him for greater things, and are currently considering a mime act. And the report says that Bernie should go up and see the results, though preferably not without warning them first. Because the squatters have been reading up on memory loss, and it seems that a sudden shock or reminder can bring everything rushing back and they would hate Clive to be unsettled in any way. At least, the report adds, not before the end of August, which is when the tourist season finishes.

EIGHT

Every day, come rain or whatever, an ancient figure which looks like it died years ago emerges from a flat over the High St newsagent and sets off to pound the pavements around town. And every day the residents of Aylesbury keep their eyes open & their ears peeled, and as soon as the figure gets within hailing distance they are moving in double-time or disappearing down alleyways and generally coming the closest there is to doing a runner bar running.

Because the ancient figure is the grieving widow of Mr Dennis 'Hokey' Stokey, who, before being ushered out, is a fairly major criminal by Wycombe standards. Indeed, such is his local fame that when Mrs Dennis Stokey retires to Aylesbury with her sorrow she is treated with much respect & credit, at least for the first month or so.

But eventually the credit runs out & the glamour wears

off, and Mrs Dennis Stokey is revealed as the most demanding and troublesome old person anyone has ever encountered, with the result that the residents try to encounter her as little as possible. In which they are helped by the fact that, when Mrs Dennis Stokey is out for her walks, she is overtaken by everything including traffic jams; because though upright, she always walks so slowly it is a miracle she is not embalmed on the spot.

Now when Mrs Dennis Stokey arrives in Aylesbury, her worldly possessions include a small & moth-eaten black dog called Rigsby, which she is forever telling people is her only friend left in the world, and which is always seen creeping along the pavement with Mrs Dennis Stokey in a loyal & resigned way. Until one day when Damage's little sister takes it for a walk and lets it off the lead in the middle of the playing fields, and apparently Rigsby takes one look at the wide open spaces and collapses, and later the vet diagnoses heart failure brought on by severe shock.

Mrs Dennis Stokey is obviously inconsolable, since a week later she reappears with another dog she calls Rigsby 2, which it seems she has been moved to save from a fate equal to death at the animal sanctuary. But Rigsby 2 is quite a different animal to its predecessor, being a large & sprightly young alsatian unused to leads or pavements; indeed for a time it is touch & go whose view on life will triumph. Many shopkeepers watching them battle it out are betting Mrs Dennis Stokey will be stumping up for roller skates in the near future, since Rigsby 2 is full of the joys of spring, and as determined to forge ahead as Mrs Dennis Stokey is determined to stop him.

But Mrs Dennis Stokey is not the widow of Dennis Stokey for nothing, having nerves of steel and even stronger sinews in her feeble frame; also she invests in a choke chain. And so after a few months Rigsby 2 can be seen creaking at a snail's pace alongside her & not lifting his head even when the local cats are dancing round him in a tempting fashion.

Across the road from Rigsby 2 and Mrs Dennis Stokey, in a little flat over the Indian, lives an acquaintance of Damage's called Larry, who shopkeepers for miles around know as Happy, as he is always beaming & cheerful with a kind word for everyone, even children. No one knows exactly what Larry has to be happy about, and this generates much puzzlement within the community, as he is the sort for whom nothing turns out right, even when it does not go wrong straight off as it generally does. Which would not matter so much if Larry were working in a bank or similar, but instead he has elected to strike a blow for personal enterprise, regarding himself as a bit of a wheeler & dealer & fixer, or in layman's terms a fence.

*   *   *

Larry is, however, a very small fence, specialising in anything people cannot shift for love or money. His flat is overflowing with old 70's records and stuffed canaries and six framed prints of blackpool pier from different angles, as well as many china thimbles, which owners would be hurt to discover are not the desirable investment once promised by the Sunday supplements. But recently Larry has been eyeing up the car market, and his first venture ends in him trying to sell a used car back to its former owner, who up until the time has not been aware that he has finished using it himself.

So Larry is hauled up in front of the local magistrate, and it is sheer misfortune that, this very morning, the magistrate has been pinned against an alley wall by Mrs Dennis Stokey, on the hunt for a resident to sort her plumbing. After the magistrate points out that plumbing is not in her line, Mrs Dennis Stokey becomes quite abusive, and when she finally leaves in search of better prey her parting words are, 'Common as muck,' which the magistrate feels is uncalled for.

So, on seeing Larry fiddling nervously with his nose-ring in the dock the magistrate's eyes gleam with sudden enthusiasm, and shortly Larry finds himself being given 120 hours' community service instead of the stretch he is expecting. Of course there is a catch, and when Larry emerges it is with a bowed head and an unusually

subdued manner, because he knows that 120 hours of
Mrs Dennis Stokey is about 119 hours and 57 mins more
than a living person can stand.

But his options are limited, so Larry puts on a brave
face, and the following Monday Mrs Dennis Stokey is
not surprised to discover him on her doorstep. Over
the weekend the authorities have had a firm word with
Mrs Dennis Stokey, having had it with weeping home
helps & volunteers arriving back in their offices almost
before they have left because Mrs Dennis Stokey has
been rejecting them on grounds ranging from haircuts
to nationalities, and this is her last in a long row of
chances.

So Larry is greeted with a sweet & resigned smile, which
becomes grimmer when it lights on the nose-ring, and
from that moment on Larry does not have time to fence
so much as an Abba tape, being kept so busy round
Mrs Dennis Stokey's that it is all he can do to crawl
home after. In fact, Larry is constantly amazed by the
tardis-like qualities of Mrs Dennis Stokey's tiny flat,
since no matter how much he scrubs floors & removes
piles of yellow newspapers there is always more waiting
for him the next morning. Yet despite this the place is
such a tight fit that Larry is practically standing on its
owner from the moment he is through the door; also
every time he turns round he finds Rigsby 2 staring at
him gloomily from his vantage point on the sofa.

After a while even Larry's cheerful nature is showing a few cracks, and his dreams have started to feature coffins or wolves or both, when one morning Mrs Dennis Stokey informs him that she has a dentist appointment, and is therefore forced to leave him alone in the flat. She adds that, in case Larry thinks he can pull a fast one she is leaving him under the supervision of Rigsby 2, and Larry is so unnerved by the idea that he does not bother protesting he is not about to pull anything, which he is not, having already noticed that, even by his standards, there is nothing worth pulling.

Once Mrs Dennis Stokey has departed, Larry steps cautiously into the sitting room with some hope of getting on Rigsby 2's good side, but it seems that Rigsby 2 no longer has a good side. No matter how much Larry frolics & gambols encouragingly in front of him, Rigsby 2 just lies sullenly with his head between his paws looking like he wishes to end Larry's frolicking personally. And eventually Larry gives up feeling somewhat foolish, and also disappointed, being fond of dogs as a rule, though he is concluding that Rigsby 2 might be the exception.

Some time later he is unenthusiastically scraping the top of Mrs Dennis Stokey's fridge when he hears the bing-bong of the door bell, so he heads into the hallway with interest, having noticed a definite absence of casual callers. On opening up he is confronted by two large & forbidding persons in brightly coloured shell-suits, who shoulder him aside abruptly and enter the sitting room without invitation, saying, 'Where is she?'

Larry politely replies Mrs Dennis Stokey is unavailable at present, and at though he indicates that he is on for taking any messages, the shell-suits indicate that they are happy to wait, by saying, 'We'll wait,' in harsh voices.

Somehow Larry suspects they are not open to discussion, so after offering tea and coffee etc, and being met with silent & discouraging stares he returns to scraping the fridge, frequently casting an eye into the sitting room to see how Rigsby 2 is taking all this. But, although the shell-suits are making free of the place, or as free as possible in the space available, Rigsby 2 remains silent and unmoving on his sofa, though Larry is rather cheered to see his expression has not warmed up any.

Time passes, and one of the shell-suits is apparently finding that standing nose-to-nose with his partner lacks interest, since he steps into the kitchen, though he retreats an inch or two at the sight of the fridge. Larry continues industriously scraping & scouring, whistling to show his unconcern, until the shell-suit says, 'Shut it,' which Larry naturally does.

After this the shell-suit advances closer, saying, 'You

a relative then, sonny?' and much as Larry wishes to dissociate himself from Mrs Dennis Stokey, he is too abashed to explain his presence so he says that, yes, he is Mrs Dennis Stokey's loving grandson. At which the shell-suit laughs long & loud, and turning to his partner invites him to share the joke; and soon both of them are going old Hokey's grandson, well I never, and wiping their eyes. And Larry is laughing politely along, though actually he has not got the punchline at all. But suddenly the shell-suits stop their guffawing and begin staring thoughtfully at Larry, and on the whole Larry thinks he would prefer to be stared at by Rigsby 2, teeth notwithstanding.

It is getting on for teatime and Mrs Dennis Stokey has still not returned, and if Larry did not have other concerns he would be worrying that she has had an accident or dental emergency or similar. But the shell-suits are looking increasingly impatient, and both of them are now breathing down his neck in the kitchen, and Larry is feeling that it is time for desperate measures. So he stretches out an arm for Rigsby 2's lead, which is hanging in the hall, saying, 'Time to walk the dog,' in a hearty sort of manner.

Larry considers that Rigsby 2 lets him down badly at this point, since he fails to bound or woof or paw the door in his excitement; instead he lets out a dull sigh & remains slumped on his sofa. In any case, it appears from the shell-suits' response that no one is going anywhere. But in the meantime Larry is gathering his courage in his hands and bending over Rigsby 2, and the following second Rigsby 2 is leaping off the sofa like a dog crazed, and bounding & yelping in a fashion guaranteed to gladden the heart of any owner. Larry says, 'See?' explaining that Rigsby 2 gets very upset if he misses his walks, and just in case the shell-suits have missed the point he surreptitiously prods Rigsby 2 with the potato peeler again. And much as Larry hates to distress any living thing, he feels that in this case the means are justified, as Rigsby 2 is now snarling & howling and generally kicking up such a fuss that the shell-suits are muttering christ in tones of despair. And when angry neighbourly bangings start filtering down from above, the shell-suits say right, that is it, since it seems they do not wish to risk someone calling the authorities.

But they add that, in case Larry has any clever ideas, they are coming along for the walk. Sadly, Larry does not, his cleverest idea being to ditch Rigsby 2 and leg it. So the procession heads for the High St, where it becomes apparent that Rigsby 2 is dictating the pace, as a bottleneck is soon building up behind them, and many pedestrians are saying tsk tsk tsk in irritation and some are saying it is a disgrace, and others are suggesting that it would be a kindness to take Rigsby 2 to a vet and leave him there. As a result the shell-suits are turning quite pink with embarrassment and saying can't you get it to go any faster? in disbelief, and Larry is replying cheerfully that he does not think even a rocket could make Rigsby 2 go any faster, when there is a slight commotion ahead of them, and the procession grinds to a sudden stop.

Because out of a crowd of fast-moving pedestrians appears Mrs Dennis Stokey, and while she creaks up to them screeching Rigsby 2 and what are you doing with him you savages? the shell-suits are gazing at her in growing puzzlement. Eventually one of them queries, 'Who is this old bat?'

Larry shakes his head at Mrs Dennis Stokey and mouths urgently, but she is of course ignoring him, and saying haughtily, 'I am Mrs Dennis Stokey.' In response the shell-suits are exclaiming that is never old Hokey's bird, apparently believing that even an aged Dennis Stokey would go for something more decorative around the house. But many protests and mutterings are still filling the air, and the shell-suits realise they are attracting undue attention, so before Larry or Mrs Dennis Stokey can murmur a word of protest they are being bundled into an illegally parked sierra, which screeches away from the pavement and is soon accelerating out of town.

Thanks to Damage, Larry is untroubled by erratic driving, though he cannot help feeling he would enjoy the ride more without Rigsby 2 on top of him. At least

Rigsby 2 is not making any crushing moves; in fact he is staring thoughtfully at the trees & cars & cows rushing by, and Larry realises this is probably his first taste of adventure since Mrs Dennis Stokey came into his life, and is eyeing Rigsby 2 somewhat apprehensively. But Rigsby 2 just continues to watch, and if he is thinking anything he is keeping it to himself.

Meanwhile the shell-suits have accepted Dennis Stokey's lapse in taste, albeit reluctantly. Since it seems from their conversation that ever since they are just boys in Wycombe Dennis Stokey is a hero and role model to them, indeed they are both shocked & saddened when they hear of his untimely exit. But after the shock wears off they realise they are prime candidates for his vacant position, with the advantage of being able to dispense with interviews and other red tape. So they step into Dennis Stokey's old shoes, and are in the process of modernising his business when rumours start circulating about a large consignment from Amsterdam which Dennis Stokey received a few days before his departure. No one knows what this consignment is, but reports suggest it is so hot that Dennis Stokey buried it in a secret location intending to retrieve it later, little realising he would shortly be late himself.

At this time business is not proving too productive for the shell-suits, and so they determine to get their hands on this consignment, no matter how mysterious or elusive it is, hoping it will solve some urgent cash-flow problems. The trouble is, by now Dennis Stokey's business has been modernised so thoroughly that there is almost no one remaining from his old crowd, and anyone accidentally left over is in hiding.

Which leaves Mrs Dennis Stokey, and although the shell-suits have been congratulating themselves on their cunning coup, now they are looking notice-ably unsettled. Because while Mrs Dennis Stokey is showing no particular distress at references to her late husband, she is objecting more than a lit-tle to the driving, and is moaning and complaining and agitating in the front seat, and prodding the driving shell-suit with her bony fingers until he is looking pleadingly to his partner for support. And whenever the shell-suits try to rise above this by discussing business matters she comments, 'Those who live by the sword die by the sword' in tones of deep satisfaction.

But eventually she tires of this, although she con-tinues to remark sarcastically on the state of the modern criminal. By the time the shell-suits have been informed that Dennis Stokey would have died before wearing nylon, and, unlike some always kept himself in condition, and moreover would never have dreamt of abducting anyone in full view of a High St, they are sinking into their seats and muttering poor old Hokey, no wonder he looked so contented in his coffin.

Presently the car pulls into what appears to be a deserted wasteland, and after carefully putting on the handbrake the driving shell-suit turns to Larry and Mrs Dennis Stokey saying, 'Out' in a voice that brooks no argument. So they get out of the car, and although Larry leaves the door open for Rigsby 2 in case he should be moved to save the day or similar, Rigsby 2 shows no such urge but continues staring out of the window in a rather stunned manner.

The shell-suits now close in on Mrs Dennis Stokey saying right, where is it? when to everyone's surprise Mrs Dennis Stokey casts off her tough exterior and begins weeping and wailing, 'I am only a poor old woman, have mercy,' quickly adding that she has no idea what they are talking about. And no matter how firmly the shell-suits twist her arm or threaten her with unspecified tortures, Mrs Dennis Stokey remains a sobbing & quivering wreck on the bracken, until the shell-suits are fast losing their enthusiasm. Indeed, when Mrs Dennis Stokey raises a tear-streaked face and says, 'What if it was your grandmother?' they lose it altogether and withdraw for urgent consultation.

Larry is standing quietly minding his own business, and hoping that whatever happens to Mrs Dennis Stokey will not be too long & protracted because he has a sensitive stomach, when to his surprise he finds himself suddenly in the centre of things. The shell-suits are explaining to Mrs Dennis Stokey that her loving grandson is about to become her loving grandson parts 1 to 4, unless of course she chooses to come clean on the consignment, at which they brandish the sharp end of a tyre iron in Larry's general direction, and look at Mrs Dennis Stokey expectantly.

But Mrs Dennis Stokey lifts her head and flatly denies any relationship to Larry, no matter how distant, so Larry seizes the opportunity to explain matters. And the shell-suits listen to his story with professional interest, occasionally interjecting with comments such as, 120 hours with her? which they also seem to feel is beyond the pale. But after Larry has finished they say, sorry son, and continue to wave the tyre iron in his face, reasoning that relative or not, Mrs Dennis Stokey will not wish the guilt of his suffering on her old shoulders.

But Mrs Dennis Stokey replies from the bracken, 'Try me,' and it rapidly becomes clear that she does not give two hoots about Larry, suffering or otherwise.

The shell-suits are nonplussed by this attitude and also somewhat repelled, and although one suggests that they try Rigsby 2, neither appears to be downcast when it turns out that Rigsby 2 has vanished. Besides, by now both of them agree that Mrs Dennis Stokey would probably have taken the tyre iron to him personally. So there is a short break, during which the shell-suits obviously decide to cut their losses, because one of them then says rather gloomily, 'Might as well be off then.' And seeing Larry shivering by the car he adds, 'Why not hop in, son? We'll see you home.'

When Mrs Dennis Stokey begins again to wail & protest she is met with deaf ears and a disbelieving stare or three, after which the car drives off leaving her alone in the middle of the wasteland. And anyone watching would see a remarkable transformation, because when the car has disappeared Mrs Dennis Stokey brushes the tears off her face and dusts down her coat, and rising from the bracken begins a slow but determined progress towards some lights twinkling in the distance.

Back in the car the atmosphere is getting convivial, since Larry considers that the shell-suits have been very gentlemanly under the circumstances, and assures them that nothing is broken when they ask. And soon cigs are being handed round, together with cans discovered in the glove compartment, and Larry is leaning forwards from the back seat so as not to miss the conversation, which mainly consists of the shell-suits exclaiming jesus what a woman and agreeing that, if Dennis Stokey had not been discovered with more holes in him than a cheese grater, they would be tempted to assume that he had shown himself out. One of them adds, 'In front of his own workbench too,' after which there is a rather melancholy pause, broken by Larry enquiring, 'Machine gun, was it?' having only vague memories of the press reports.

The shell-suits reply no with some animation, since it seems that Dennis Stokey's dramatic end is caused by his own drill. It has been the talk of Wycombe for months, because both the drill & the driller disappear into thin air, and despite the best efforts of the law, and here the shell-suits laugh rather unkindly, they are never found.

Larry is saying no and really? followed by here will do, as they are nearing the region of Mrs Dennis Stokey's home and he wishes to pick up his stuff. On hearing this the shell-suits prick up their ears, and they are soon following Larry up the stairs and through the door, saying that they might as well take a proper look. But there is still no sign of the consignment. Meanwhile Larry is reclining on the sofa, which for once is free of Rigsby 2's offputting presence, and beginning to wish the shell-suits would hurry it up a bit, though of course he does not say so.

Finally the shell-suits take their leave, and on their way out they bend down to shake Larry's hand, reminding

him to get in touch if he hears anything about the consignment, at which request their eyes narrow slightly
and the handshakes get noticeably firmer. And Larry
replies in a suitable vein, but he is fretting inwardly, and
as soon as the shell-suits are out of the door he leaps off
the sofa like Rigsby 2 before him and pulls off cushions
with abandon.

Because all the time he has been reclining, Larry has
heard a quiet rustling underneath him, and sure enough
he is soon gazing at a large black bin-liner, which it
seems has been doubling as sofa stuffing. When he
rips it open Larry sees hundreds and thousands of little
white pills, which he suspects may be e, but which he
is sensibly not about to try and confirm until he has
reached the safety of his flat. In fact, tests subsequently
show Larry is the proud new owner of some of the best
stuff around, and even after a fine time is had by all
proving it, Larry makes enough to retire from fencing
for ever.

But at the moment Larry is naturally more concerned
with retiring from Mrs Dennis Stokey's flat before she
finds her way back to it; and it is only when he is in
his own sitting room, examining the haul at his leisure,
that he finds the bag also contains a battered old black
& decker, which seems to have gone somewhat rusty
around the edges.

*   *   *

Larry looks at it in silence for a bit, since he is not slow on the uptake, and is soon thinking how unpleasant things would be for Mrs Dennis Stokey if the shell-suits got wind of this new find. And presently he takes an equally thoughtful stroll round the block, and when he returns the drill is in a skip outside Sainsbury's while Larry is humming quietly like a man with 120 hours of community service lifted from his shoulders.

But meanwhile, in a wasteland somewhere outside Aylesbury, Mrs Dennis Stokey is grimly struggling on, and even were she aware of Larry's discovery it is likely she would dismiss it as somewhat trivial. Since for some time now her journey has been interrupted by a disused gravel pit, and not being au fait with public safety films Mrs Dennis Stokey has been surprised to find the pit full of deceptively deep water; also there seem to be several supermarket trolleys and old bedsteads and so on lying in ambush beneath the surface.

So for some time Mrs Dennis Stokey has been splashing around and crying for help, and she is reaching the end of her tether when she notices an outline on the dark horizon. And as the outline gets closer it seems to Mrs Dennis Stokey to be Rigsby 2, although if it is it is a new version, because this one is currently frolicking and gambolling and barking with canine delight, and is running up hillocks like a young lamb in spring and down them like a rocket train.

But when the outline hears Mrs Dennis Stokey's voice it stops dead in its tracks. And Mrs Dennis Stokey is still splashing and almost despairing, but now she takes heart and, wrestling off a bedstead, shouts, 'Come here.'

Rigsby 2 obediently turns, and Mrs Dennis Stokey sees him stand and shiver, and then Rigsby 2 begins moving towards her, but he is not running. Instead his head goes down and his tail hangs between his legs, and he is creaking very very slowly towards her, and with each slow step he takes Mrs Dennis Stokey is sinking further and further into the pit's embrace. And although every time she surfaces she is screaming at Rigsby 2 to get a move on, Rigsby 2 continues to creak along, and by the time he gets there Mrs Dennis Stokey is nowhere in sight.

N I N E

Late one night, Guy enters the Kings Head & sits without a word, but it is general knowledge that he has just clocked up his annual visit to his grandparent, so everyone is understanding. And their minds turn to higher matters, but to widespread surprise Guy suddenly begins to speak; and it seems that, while he is fretting & pacing & watching the clock go tick tick tick very slowly, his grandparent embarks on a story; and the story, or as near as Guy remembers it, is as follows.

Way, way back, not long after a world war kicks off, there is a small family living off the fat of the land in darkest Buckinghamshire. And in the cities there are bombs banging and the blitz blazing and everyone insisting we'll meet again despite all the evidence, but meanwhile this family is enjoying rustic peace with as much veg as they can eat, and can therefore be expected to be reasonably content under the circs, if somewhat backward.

*　　*　　*

But of course things are never this simple. Even in this rural idyll there is strife & heartbreak & deprivation and so on, and much of it is caused by the family patriarch, who doubles as the local vicar, and who by the sounds of it is on something of a power kick. Indeed it seems that his family feel the bombing & blitzing would rate as light entertainment by comparison, because when they are not mending ploughshares or toiling in the fields or giving thanks for their potatoes, they are sweating over psalms and reciting tables and conjugating verbs, the vicar being a firm believer in the merits of education. And though he always informs his family that they will be grateful to him in later life, privately they have increasing doubts about this.

Now somehow this vicar has managed to acquire children, and the youngest is a sad trial & a disappointment to him. In fact he is known to his brothers & sisters by the odd name of Wages, since from day one his father greets him with the cheery expression 'The wages of sin is death' as a general reminder. But it never has the desired effect, and Wages continues to skive & scrap and torment his sisters with dead frogs and dried peas and so on. And one morning the family wakes to find that Wages has departed in the night, on which discovery his father is heard to say, 'The Lord moves in mysterious ways,' after which the rest of the family are requested to drop the subject.

Guy says it sounds like Wages has his head screwed on more than most kids, as while his distraught mother is sobbing into her mash and his brothers & sisters are gloomily forking over the cabbages, Wages is stowed away on a troop train and already half-way to London, having decided that this is where the action is. And soon he is making his way through what is left of the east end, and all around him are wailing sirens and wailing kids being packed off to the countryside, and Wages is looking at them with some sympathy and thinking that they do not yet know the half of it.

In those days apparently the east end is much the same as it is today i.e. full of gangsters & pimps and so on, and the first door Wages knocks on is opened by a skinny female not fitted with the standard heart of gold, since she says, 'Get lost,' and slams the door in his face. But Wages continues along the street telling himself that the lord will provide in a somewhat defiant manner, this being one of his father's least favourite quotations. And sure enough he is shortly swinging his heels in a chirpy cockney pub warbling knees up mother brown or whatever, and being made much of by the clientele, who are flattered & amazed that such a small kid should embark on such a large journey, Buckinghamshire being all of forty miles away.

And while he is wolfing down eels & pies and noticing

with relief that there is not a vegetable in sight, Wages is boasting more than a little of his adventure and explaining how he has come to his decision to travel. The clientele listen to his tales of lessons and catechisms with many shudders of horror and sympathy, until a dapper sort of punter with a moustache resembling a caterpillar leans forward to speak, at which the rest of the pub immediately become like clams.

'Wages,' says this person into the hush, Wages having requested everyone to call him by this handle, 'can you speak French?'

Wages says, 'Oui,' quite proudly, though finding this goes down like double dutch he then translates accordingly.

'Wages,' says this person, 'I think I have a job for you,' and he looks round with a broad smile, at which all of the pub smirk sycophantically back. And shortly after the person downs his pint and encourages Wages to follow suit with whatever kids are drinking back then, possibly beetroot juice. So Wages does and soon he is trotting off down the cobbled alleyways after his prospective employer, who en route says that Wages can call him Reg. And Wages says pleased to meet you, and Reg says likewise, and the journey passes in this fashion until they arrive at a little two-up on a back-street abutting the river.

*   *   *

The door is opened by a female sporting sagging hair &
baggy eyes and an even more relaxed negligée, so Wages
reckons this must be what his father terms a loose
woman, and consequently greets her with enthusiasm
& interest. But the female ignores him, instead greeting
Reg with, 'What the bleedin blue blazes is this then?'
or similar.

Reg explains that the kid speaks french, which does not
seem much of an explanation to Wages, but it magically
transforms the female into one hugging him to her
ample bosom crying come in come in my little lamb
Auntie Edith will get you a cup o char. Wages does not
really want a cup o char but he comes in regardless, and
while he is cautiously sipping Reg slaps the proposed
deal on the table, with many sidelong glances at Auntie
Edith to check it is all in order & understood.

The deal, Reg begins, is a piece of cake, and one which a
bright young fellow like Wages should have no trouble
swallowing. But it is, he adds, a sad & moving story,
so if Wages is by any chance soft hearted or weak
stomached he should speak now or forever shut it.
Wages replies with indignation that he is neither, at
which Reg says he is relieved to hear it.

Upstairs, Reg continues, there is a very unhappy man,
who is, and here he pauses for a long second in thought,

Auntie Edith's long-lost French brother Henri. Before Wages can speak Reg adds smartly that they are separated at birth, that is how, and a week ago last Tuesday this Henri turns up out of the blue on his sister's doorstep without an onion to his name and in a state of Gallic distress. Of course all Auntie Edith wishes is to see him happy & smiling like the chubby little cherub of which she has such fond if distant memories.

Now the problem with this Reg says, is the language barrier. Henri, while being occasionally vocal, especially after a nip or so, is always vocal in the wrong vernacular, and in the east end people do not go much for speaking in tongues. Indeed, Reg says, he (Reg), can muster only one French word to his name and that is letter. At this both Reg and Auntie Edith perform a couple of sniggers before returning to the main agenda.

All Wages is required to do, Reg says, is offer Henri the odd kind word, check he is getting enough to drink and so on, and maybe translate a few very simple instructions which Reg will be supplying. And in return Wages will get as much as he can eat & a bob a day on top, not to mention a free trip back home in Reg's spanking new motor should he so desire.

Wages muses for a nano-second before replying you bet, and Reg & Auntie Edith visibly relax, but still Reg asks somewhat anxiously whether he thinks his French is up to it. Wages replies oh I think so, and in fact he is sure of it, languages being the one thing he takes to like a boat to barnacles, though he does not like to flaunt this achievement.

Next thing he knows, Reg is unbolting a creaky old door at the end of a corridor, explaining that Henri is the excitable type so they do not encourage him to roam, at least not without supervision. And seeing Wages look taken aback, Reg adds cheerfully that there is no need to worry, since currently Henri is tranked up to the eyeballs if not beyond, after which he coughs & says well, anyway.

The door groans open and Wages sees a dark & stubbly shape in a dim corner, and Reg says all right Henri in loud & breezy tones. In reply, the shape spits heavily on the floor and says euh. Reg seems to welcome this, since he turns to Wages and says go on then, say hello.

Wages obediently says allo, at which Reg is going is that it? in some disappointment. But on detecting the accents of his native land the shape lets loose a torrent of euhs followed by a deluge of ahs & ers, though Wages does not think they mean anything, let alone French. On being informed of this, Reg mutters well, maybe Edith overdoes the dose a bit, and they back out of the room, Reg locking it and stowing the key carefully on the door ledge.

Come the morning, Wages is kicking his heels thoughtfully over the side of the thames, and after he scores two seagulls & a barge captain with his brekky apple cores he wanders down the alleys on the scent of further info. Because a mystery to Wages is as a red double-blanket to a bull, and something is telling him that Reg is not completely sincere in his explanations; indeed he is smelling something fishy a mile off upwind.

Soon Wages finds himself deep in conversation with a friendly organ-grinder, and while they are strolling underneath the arches etc, Wages notices a small figure promenading ahead of them, and is puzzled to see it is attracting as much interest from the natives as if it is a glamour model, which it is not, appearing even at a distance short & dumpy and not a looker in any sense. But the organ-grinder informs Wages with civic pride that this is not just any old pedestrian, rather it is a local landmark & monument going under the name of Miss April Ashby.

Now Miss April Ashby is renowned far & wide for her charm and graceful airs, and also for her bank balance, which is loaded. Fortunately for Miss April Ashby this financial advantage does not damage her prestige in the locality one iota; on the contrary, she is much beloved by all since she is dishing it out as fast as it comes in, if not faster. And Wages learns that he is within spitting distance of the Miss April Ashby Childrens Trust and the Miss April Ashby Home for the Walking Wounded, not to mention the Miss April Ashby chain of dosshouses & soup kitchens; indeed, she is practically a one-woman franchise.

Ahead of them Miss April Ashby is going her way with many kind words and a groat or so for each & every beggar. Wages sees that many of them are becoming quite carried away by this generosity and are throwing their caps in the air & shouting hip hip hooray for Miss April Ashby in a fawning manner, and that Miss April Ashby is looking rather embarrassed by this, as if she wishes they would cut it out but is too polite to say so. And after they have overtaken her, Wages mutters she is all right I suppose, but this is an unconvincing bluff, since Wages has fallen hook line & sinker for Miss April Ashby's big brown Jersey eyes just like everyone else in her vicinity.

But the organ-grinder sadly informs him that, despite this apparently universal appeal there is still one person who always looks at Miss April Ashby with envy & fury & other such negative and destructive emotions. In fact it transpires that Wages is currently living with him, because it is none other than Miss April Ashby's wicked cousin Reg, who does not have Miss April

Ashby's many plus points, having been born on the wrong side of a blanket though what this means & why it should affect his character, Guy adds, he does not have the faintest.

Whatever, Reg has been left to make his own way in life, and is doing so quite energetically, having his finger in many pies, most of them unsavoury. But it seems that he still covets Miss April Ashby's bank balance no end, and, being her only living relative, it is well within his grasp. But Miss April Ashby is always in the rudest of health without so much as a sniffle in winter, which is proving a source of great chagrin & disappointment to her cousin, though he is careful not to show it.

Because Miss April Ashby is the unworldly sort, and is naive & trusting like many young females when it comes to family matters. Indeed not long before she has made out a will leaving everything in Reg's favour, and as a result the community is not trusting Reg as far as they can throw him, i.e. about four feet. Instead they are supervising him like a neighbourhood watch scheme, and the organ-grinder adds that there is no shortage of volunteers, because if Reg gets his hands on Miss April Ashby's bank balance no one else will see a penny of it, and they can all kiss goodbye to the groats & soup kitchens etc, which they are naturally unwilling to do.

The result is that Reg cannot move an inch without bumping into a loitering pearly king or pie seller; and with Reg taken care of, Miss April Ashby's continuing well-being is assured. Because, the organ-grinder declares with some emotion, he does not know what other person would ever contemplate some dastardly deed upon her person, but they would have to be a pretty low-down specimen, since even the east end's hardest cases do not dream of harming a hair on Miss April Ashby's little head. Apparently, Reg has discovered this also, as he is recently heard to be making enquiries.

At this point Wages takes his leave with many sensations burning in his boyish breast, as he is now seeing himself as Sherlock Holmes or Dick Tracy or preferably the Sweeney though it is not yet invented. And late that night a small & determined figure creeps quietly along the corridor of Reg's two-up and eases a key down with the help of a broom handle.

Soon Wages is standing inside Henri's room with his heart pounding, and about to hiss wake up in the best french he can muster, when with dramatic irony Reg's voice chooses this moment to filter down through the floorboards. So Wages stops and listens, and within minutes his worst suspicions are unfolding into his eardrums, because in their bedroom Reg & Auntie Edith are chatting heedless of their danger, and occasionally clinking glasses to the success of their devilish and fairly cunning plan.

As the truth of the situation dawns on him, Wages's jaw sets with grim determination, because Reg & Auntie Edith are planning on using Henri as a waste disposal unit, and of course the waste they wish to dispose of is Miss April Ashby. But it seems that before Wages turns up on the scene they are stumped. Although Henri originally turns up complete with a willing compatriot, as soon as they sign up to Reg's retirement scheme Henri decides to increase his profit margins and lays off his compatriot in a decisive manner, in fact with one of Auntie Edith's kitchen knives.

Which is rather foolish, as the compatriot is acting as translator, and his rash action leaves Henri in the dark about who & when & where and so on, though there is no doubting his general commitment. So Wages's arrival is as manna from heaven to Reg & Auntie Edith. On top of everything else they have been finding it increasingly tiresome keeping Henri on ice in the meantime, and from what Wages can hear of Auntie Edith's critical commentary upstairs, he gathers that Henri is neither her brother nor anything like it. Indeed, it seems that she and Reg have not an earthly who he is, and neither do they seem inclined to find out, being of the opinion Henri is the nastiest piece of work they have ever come across.

Following this Wages hears Reg saying what about the kid? and Auntie Edith's voice replying it is fine, he is just a baby and a country one at that, to which Reg jovially replies ooh ar ooh ar, having obviously clichéd notions of provincial life. After which there is silence, broken only by the gentle twanging of bedsprings in the night.

Wages's jaw sets even more grimly at this, and he attacks Henri's ear with some urgency, and soon Henri is ungluing his eyeballs with a dazed & confused air. But Wages does not have an opportunity to entice Henri off his evil path as he is planning, because as soon as Henri becomes compos mentis he lunges for Wages's throat in the manner of a pit bull, and Wages finds to his dismay that he can utter nothing but a short squawk.

Next he is propelled out of the two-up and down an alley, and if Wages had taken to Henri, which he has not, chances are he would be feeling more than a little sorry for him, since Henri is demonstrating a serious case of cabin fever, having spent weeks in his little room without so much as a wireless to while away the hours, and is looking wildly around him and muttering mon dieu at regular intervals. And though his hand is still clamped to Wages's shoulder, Wages notices the fingers vibrating as if with palsy, and out of the corner of his eye he sees that Henri is much less mature than

his impressive reputation suggests; indeed, he looks to
be of an age with Wages's largest brother, though there
the resemblance stops in its tracks. Because the further
they get down the street the more Henri's character
emerges, and it is not a christian one. In fact he is
shortly kicking over a passing cripple's crutches and
soon after helps himself to a beggar's meagre takings,
not looking at all repentant but laughing evilly at both
events.

After this Henri raises his nose and sniffs, since wafting
on the breeze comes the scent of running bitter and
maybe a crisp or two. And though up to this moment
Henri has not addressed a word to Wages, he now
grunts, 'Translate,' in his direction, before pulling him
into the pub.

As they pass through the door Henri swaggers and displays his shoulders and generally gives it the large like
a fighting cockerel, but none of the clientele comments
on this approach. Instead, the cheery shouts of roll out
the barrel and how's your father rapidly die away until
Wages and Henri are surrounded by a sea of large and
unsmiling faces, which are gazing at Henri's stripey
T-shirt and J'aime Maman tattoo with some suspicion.

After a moment this standoff is interrupted by Henri
clearing his throat, and Wages sees with some trepidation that he is about to speak.

'Tell them,' he says to Wages, and Wages does not understand the following phrases, his French being of the classical era, but he gets the general drift without difficulty.

So Henri sits back with an expectant expression and flexes his biceps, and Wages takes a deep breath and begins to translate, and the next moment Henri is surrounded by punters cheering and slapping him on the shoulder and placing foaming pints on his table, because Wages's translation has not been one hundred per cent accurate. Indeed it seems to have left the clientele with the strong impression that Henri considers the British a breed of heroes, and that his first visit is making him deeply ashamed of his French background for the first time in his natural. After which Wages adds rule britannia and other such sentiments for good measure, and despite his fears that he may have overdone things the punters are now glowing like windscale with honest pride & patriotism.

Henri is obviously somewhat stymied by this response, but although his biceps are twitching angrily he is finding bevvies pressed into his hand before he can follow through. Besides, every time he snarls espèce de con, Wages tactfully reruns this as you are all so kind; what have I done to deserve this great british hospitality? And all of a sudden Henri shrugs & lifts the nearest bevvy, at which all the punters opine good on you and wave their pints back in a friendly way, and after a period a rusty smile is seen to be edging its way across Henri's lips. And by the time Henri wins at dominoes and is runner-up at darts and is deciding to call it a night, Wages finds himself translating, 'Thank you,' without any improvisation necessary.

Now Wages sees great possibilities in this situation, especially when both Reg and Miss April Ashby leave the area on business, though in different counties. Night after night he calls for Henri as arranged, and by the end of the week Henri is bouncing into the local & slapping backs without prompting and otherwise blossoming like a cherry tree.

And one night, he and Wages are wandering back to the two-up, with Henri confiding to Wages that he has never had such a time in his life, since in his homeland everyone greets him with suspicion & aggro from day one, as a result of which he is always getting in first with a bottle or similar to be on the safe side. After this declaration Henri prances up to a passing beggar and donates him a farthing out of his darts winnings, and then looks proudly at Wages to see how he is greeting this transformation.

But Wages is deep in thought, since while he is becoming fonder of Henri than seems possible given the circs, he is really sticking with the situation for the sake of Miss April Ashby and her big brown jerseys. To his dismay, every time he raises this delicate subject Henri shrugs expressively and replies that, all things being equal and with recent events in mind, he would drop this Miss April Ashby termination like a shot, though he had never thought to see the day where he would be saying this.

But, and here Henri looks faintly troubled yet decisive, he is bound by honour & contractual obligations to continue. Not only that, but he is planning to retire on the proceeds; indeed it is his dream to buy a little piece of land on the riviera and spend his days farming in a peaceful & organic fashion. Following which he brightens up & slaps Wages on the back, saying, 'You cannot make an omelette without breaking eggs,' and although Wages knows this to be true, he is not comforted.

It is looking like the only solution is to shop Henri to the locals, but Wages does not fancy this, since he knows that Henri would not last five minutes once the news is out. Wages is examining his options with some urgency, because both Reg and Miss April Ashby are due back in town any minute, when all at once a short & compact figure pulls out of an alley and starts beetling down the road towards them.

From the gruel-laden basket it is carrying and its general air of joie de vivre, Wages recognises Miss April Ashby, and he is thanking heaven Henri has no idea what she looks like. Otherwise he suspects her joie de vivre would be somewhat short-lived. But Henri's nose is pointing towards the figure with interest, being french, and he is muttering une femme to himself enthusiastically, having been solely restricted to male company over the last weeks, unless you include Auntie Edith, which obviously he does not.

Wages starts saying brightly gosh look at that fascinating chimney stack and creating other such distractions, but Miss April Ashby continues to attract Henri's gaze like a magnet. When all at once she throws up her hands and lets out a little cry, and Wages sees her disappear under half a dozen or so vagrant types who appear to have been lurking behind a bollard. This is obviously a case of mistaken identity; but before her attackers can recognise Miss April Ashby and realise their error and apologise Henri is on them like an avenging angel. All Wages can do is sit back and watch, since Henri is leaping in with shouts of joy & an air of having missed this kind of exercise more than a little, and soon he is juggling several vagrants at once and swinging them round like dumb-bells and after about twelve seconds the only things left on the pavement are Miss April Ashby and her basket, and at least one of them is looking up at Henri with some admiration.

Henri is standing over her flushed with success & manly pride, although when Wages rushes over, all he can say is, 'What does this stupid girl do out at night anyway?' and with a sinking feeling Wages realises that, though Henri may have come a long way since their first meeting, he is still very far from charm school.

So, mentally crossing his fingers, Wages embarks on another translation. He is explaining to Miss April Ashby that Henri hopes she is not unduly distressed and by the way what remarkable eyes she has, when to his horror Miss April Ashby opens her mouth and emits a stream of perfect French, and the first thing she says is, 'You are right. It was very foolish.'

And Wages sees for the first time that Miss April Ashby is looking at Henri with extreme interest. Indeed she is ignoring Wages completely. She says to Henri how refreshing it is to meet someone who is not buttering her up or otherwise laying it on thick, and Henri replies oh really in a cool manner, but is gazing into her eyes like a man poleaxed. And immediately he insists on walking Miss April Ashby home.

So Wages trails somewhat sulkily behind them, kicking the kerb at intervals, and when they reach Miss April Ashby's townhouse he finds himself waiting outside rather longer than it takes to consume a coffee, though when Henri finally emerges the first thing he does is apologise, and Wages forgives him.

Because Henri is clutching Miss April Ashby's hand in a tender grasp, and Miss April Ashby is clutching him back again, and Wages hears that over their coffee Henri and Miss April Ashby discover they have many things in common, and one of them is that they have fallen head over heels with each other at first sight. Although Henri has at first kept his distance, being constrained by thoughts of his dark & murky past, Miss April Ashby roundly informs him that she gives less than a fig for his past, after which she launches herself into his arms like a bullet, and within seconds is agreeing to be his constant companion, or wife. Indeed, Henri tells Wages that her faith is not misplaced, since the way Miss April Ashby is making him feel, he never wishes to harm even a vegetable as long as he lives.

But just as Wages is retiring to give the loving couple room to manoeuvre, as they are now gazing at each other in a soupy & somewhat embarrassing fashion, there comes an infuriated cry from the sidelines. And before Henri can move a muscle Miss April Ashby is struggling and kicking in the grasp of a raging Reg, who is holding a large bayonet to her jugular and crying, 'Oh yes and he gets the money does he?' adding not on your nellie, and that he will swing for it first and so on.

Things appear to be hopeless, with Henri paralysed by this threat to his beloved, and Reg seemingly intent on making sure of his inheritance there and then, when suddenly Wages remembers his trusty peashooter, which he always keeps in his back pocket for emergencies. And the next minute Reg is reeling back with surprise and clutching his right eye and yelling ow, after which Henri makes short work of trussing him up like a turkey.

And at the wedding which soon follows Wages is guest of honour, and before the happy couple depart for Miss April Ashby's country farm, where they eventually raise many vegetables & kids & also prize jerseys, they both give long & emotional speeches saying that Wages has a standing invitation to visit whenever he wishes, because as far as they are concerned Wages has saved the day. And everyone present agrees with them.

And here, Guy says, the story ends, because his grandparent dozes off at this point, but it is not hard to imagine everyone concerned living happily ever after, that being the kind of story it is. But oddly Guy does not look any cheered by this and the community are asking why, since it is obvious that Wages is none other than Guy's grandparent and they are wishing their own grandparents had been similarly heroic instead of spending most of their lives in a coma or knitting.

But Guy remains downcast, and it appears that his grandparent is not Wages at all but Reg, who, long before he ends up as the dulux rep for the Aylesbury area, learns the whole story from Miss April Ashby when she kindly visits him in the local penitentiary.

T E N

Now not long after everyone hears the tale of Guy's grandparent, another April Ashby appears on the horizon, so of course everyone agrees that this is very strange and starts expecting a third, in the manner of buses.

But this April Ashby does not resemble the earlier model at all, having long red hair and sparky blue eyes and a chassis like a fire engine; in fact she is stacked in all areas apart from those financial, where it seems she is flat busted. And the mystery about April Ashby is why she has come to Aylesbury in the first place, because no matter how much she wanders the streets they are never paved with gold, unless you count special brew cans.

But even in Aylesbury April Ashby finds compensations, as the men are drawn in her direction like moths to a flame; and indeed she chews them up and spits them out like so many insects, and after only a few months April Ashby is running out of beds & bodies & meal tickets, and having to reassess her options.

At this point April Ashby's eye lights on a character called Normal Malarkey. It is a wonder she has not noticed him sooner because, thanks to his parents being written off by an astra, Normal Malarkey now has everything going for him, chiefly their little basement flat and its contents to call his very own. And also he looks like someone who inherits an ironing board, being spick & span and crisply buttoned down, even first thing in the a.m.

Apart from these assets, the only noteworthy thing about Normal Malarkey is his name. He is nothing much to look at, and never drinks or does anything of interest that anyone can think of, and as far as drug use goes is sounding like a government campaign and never seems discouraged by the fact that he has about the same effect. So it is widely agreed that Normal Malarkey is more normal than is natural, and as a result he is generally left to get on with it in solitary.

But April Ashby is not about to be deterred by the above, having enough going on herself for a whole funfair, and she is soon bearing Normal Malarkey into the Kings Head triumphant. Soon after this she moves herself into Normal Malarkey's home & castle, and it is not long before he starts displaying all the signs of poverty and exhaustion generally associated with the April Ashby experience, and more besides.

Because none of April Ashby's former escorts and bankrolls makes the mistake of falling for her, even if they are appreciating her company more than a little but within seconds of her murmuring how about it to Normal Malarkey he is falling like an employment figure, and is informing the world that he loves April Ashby & always will. Moreover, he seems to take much pride in this new & unusual aspect of his character, which in my opinion is foolish of Normal Malarkey, April Ashby not being the kind of person you wish to be loving unless you also wish to be counting your fingers after.

And sure enough April Ashby suddenly exits from Normal Malarkey's basement at the speed of light, together with many trinkets and family heirlooms, and no one including Normal Malarkey is able to see her for dust. And for a while all the girls in the area are doleful and in sympathy at this romantic failure but they soon get over it, and naturally expect Normal Malarkey to do likewise.

But when Normal Malarkey discovers that April Ashby has gone awol it seems he sits on his sofa and cries like a baby, because rightly or whatever, Normal Malarkey feels he is nothing without April Ashby and still loves her and is certain he always will.

After which episode Normal Malarkey throws aside all restraint and for the first time in his natural he embarks on something of a bender. It is obviously quite an epic as benders go, because when he finally straightens out days or possibly years later he is cutting a pungent & shirtless figure, with only very hazy memories of who or what he is bending with and where. Indeed, he is somewhat pushed to recollect where his home is, having been out of it & things generally for so long, and even when he totters towards his own keyhole he is still questioning his memory with suspicion.

But there is a good reason for this. Since in the course of things Normal Malarkey's front door seems to have acquired many extra locks & bolts & bars, and though Normal Malarkey is not at all against locks and bolts in principle he is naturally taken aback by the discovery they have been breeding in his absence.

But then the thought hits him that April Ashby must have returned in the interim, since she holds the only other set of keys, which Normal Malarkey has presented to her with some ceremony attached to a heart-shaped keyring. At this notion Normal Malarkey's own heart begins leaping in the manner of a landed fish, and he opens the letterbox like a birthday present and for some time yodels April down the hallway, but the hallway remains empty & silent.

Soon Normal Malarkey is yodelling with increasing desperation and also pleading & begging and rattling the doorknob. So when the door finally swings open it is like Glastonbury and the world cup rolled into one, or whatever would be Normal Malarkey's equivalent, and he shouts, 'April' and falls into the outstretched arms before him with sobs of gratitude.

But the outstretched arms are not attached to April Ashby or anyone close. On the contrary, the specimen at the door is several storeys high and many wide and the wrong sex. And it is asking Normal Malarkey in tones of outrage whether he wishes to attract the eye of the law or what, after which Normal Malarkey finds himself ushered off his own doorstep at breakneck speed.

After a minute Normal Malarkey picks himself out of the gutter and returns to the attack, but this time he is standing back with a dust-bin lid held protectively in front of him, and before the specimen can utter a word Normal Malarkey explains that he wishes only to see April Ashby. And as he says this Normal Malarkey is wearing an expression of love and grim determination like that of a born-again christian, so he is quite a disconcerting sight.

The specimen seems to catch on quite quickly, since it says, 'A bird?'

Normal Malarkey agrees that April Ashby is, though a rare and exotic one, and after hearing her general description the specimen ponders and replies that there might be something of that nature inside and it will just go & check.

So Normal Malarkey waits with his heart pounding, until the specimen returns and Normal Malarkey hears with disbelief that April Ashby does not wish to see him; in fact her exact words appear to be get lost. And the specimen adds that there is nothing doing, you know women, after which the door slams shut leaving Normal Malarkey out with the cold & dustbins.

Now Normal Malarkey cannot believe that April Ashby would not wish to see him. When they first become an item she utters many flattering comments about Normal Malarkey's appeal & prowess and so on, and though these comments soon wither and dry up Normal Malarkey prefers to forget this. So with a faithful sigh he settles down beside a nearby stack of council bins and begins watching the basement entrance, reckoning that April Ashby will have to exit sometime, if only for a pint of milk or similar. Many wet hours and cold breezes pass by with April Ashby remaining internal, and soon Normal Malarkey's teeth are chattering like a female, but he grits them and continues to watch the basement's comings & goings in an eagle-eyed fashion.

After a time he begins to wonder if April Ashby is holding an open day and, if so, how his hall carpet will stand it because the basement's entrance is like Clapham Junction, with bodies arriving in tense & miserable moods and despairing at any delay. Though by the time they emerge they look like they have won at Waterloo, it being general knowledge that Normal Malarkey's former home has become something of a crack house, an amenity which Aylesbury has previously lacked. And from behind his bins, Normal Malarkey gathers this info from the conversation of two passing customers, and as it sinks in his heart slumps and his knees begin knocking, because he knows all about crack houses and the misery and the headlines & column inches they invariably cause.

But what April Ashby is doing inside one he cannot imagine. Nevertheless, his duty is staring him sternly in the face, so Normal Malarkey creaks into an upright position and makes his way straight to the local police retreat. But the closer he gets the harder it becomes to imagine a free spirit such as April Ashby being overwhelmed with gratitude when confronted by the forces of law & order, so it is a tormented & doubtful figure which finally weaves past the old alkies being carried in and interviewees being carried out, and through the station entrance.

Eventually it makes its way in an uncertain fashion towards the desk, where it is seen to pause and mutter April forgive me before leaning over & confiding that it has something to report.

After which there is an extended silence, and the desk sergeant then looks up and catches sight of Normal Malarkey for the first time. He does not seem thrilled by the discovery, since by now Normal Malarkey is shivering & shaking as if in a high wind, though it is only fever & exposure; also his spell by the bins has not added to his overall appeal by more than a stray cabbage leaf or two. And the desk sergeant says, 'Yes?' followed after a pause by, 'Take your time, we've got all week,' in heavy sarcasm and Normal Malarkey licks his lips and looks to the ceiling for guidance and then whispers, 'Oh nothing,' and backs off to his bins like a broken man.

And presently the community are forgetting the whole business. But one evening Guy & I are en route to the Bell when a ghostly apparition emerges from the shadows and clutches Guy by the elbow with a skinny hand, and on closer examination under a street light it starts to look something like Normal Malarkey.

*   *   *

Guy & I restrain our curiosity and say how are you doing, and Normal Malarkey replies fine, fine with a ghastly smile. He is well over April Ashby; indeed he has practically forgotten her name already, and though he has had a bit of a rough time he is now wishing only to return to normality, which Guy & I say politely that we are pleased to hear, though looking at him as he stands it is difficult to see how he will achieve this.

'Oh yes,' says Normal Malarkey. 'Sadly though, I am having a cash-flow problem at the moment.' But all he needs, he continues when Guy & I do not enquire further, is a small income to get his foot on the rung again, after which he will be climbing the ladder and everything will be peaches.

Following this dubious statement, Normal Malarkey says he hopes business is going well, and Guy & I agree cautiously that it is, mainly thanks to Larry's pills which we are selling on for a small percentage. And Normal Malarkey then tells us that he wishes to cut himself in on some of our business, and on hearing this Guy & I can hardly contain our astonishment, knowing that Normal Malarkey is formerly very moral & dismissive of such issues; and consequently we realise that he must be desperate to suggest such a thing, and do not get any satisfaction at all from this sudden U-turn.

*   *   *

But since it is no skin off our noses, and because Normal Malarkey looks to be down to his last legs or maybe one, we agree to order in some extra charlie, which Normal Malarkey can then take for his own and sell on & thus enjoy a few of life's pleasures, as in this respect dealing is no different from any other employment though with more appreciative customers.

Normal Malarkey says cheers and sheds tears of gratitude, even after Guy & I add many warnings that this is a one-off, and that he should not think himself free to set up a rival company or similar; though really we are trusting him like a brother. Or on reflection not like a brother, Normal Malarkey being widely perceived as the old-fashioned type & straight as a die, which qualities are sadly lacking in most brothers of our acquaintance.

So Normal Malarkey is shortly collecting his charlie and disappearing into the night with a wild look about him, and for a time Guy & I await his return somewhat anxiously, since of course Normal Malarkey has taken it all on credit. And then we are waiting with some annoyance, and after a longer while Guy enrols several Aylesbury skins to search for Normal Malarkey, saying that this is beyond a joke, not that it was ever much of one.

*   *   *

But of Normal Malarkey there is hide nor hair, and soon it is generally agreed that he must be using the proceeds to go after April Ashby. All the girls are going ah and thinking it is very romantic, but Guy & I are deeply saddened and feel that it will be a long time before we trust again, and are only thankful that in the end we give Normal Malarkey nothing but wizz, so our loss is not as bad as it might be, though of course any loss is bad enough.

Now when Normal Malarkey scuttles off down the street with what he thinks is charlie he is innocent of the difference, but he is about to discover it. And while Guy & I would not say that he deserves what is coming to him, Normal Malarkey's plan is a low-down one in anyone's book, since he has never had any intention of making good his credit, and does not spare Guy & I so much as a twinge of conscience once he is up & running.

Because Normal Malarkey loves April Ashby & always will; indeed for some reason he loves her more than ever, and old acquaintances are but specks in his eyes compared to the log that is April Ashby's well formed figure. His only desire is to enter his former home and recover April Ashby, to which end it seems he is plotting beside his bins for days. And as Normal Malarkey finally weaves up to his old front door he is cackling feverishly at his cunning plan, since this time he bears gifts, and so he is counting on quite a different reception.

As luck would have it, he arrives during something of a dry patch, as within seconds he is standing in what remains of his kitchen, and if the assembled residents are looking at him with something close to horror, they are diplomatic enough to disguise it. So Normal Malarkey sneaks off, and is soon wandering the rooms calling April like a foghorn, but before he can get round to searching the cupboards the residents discover that what they are attempting to boil up in the kitchen is merely wizz, at which stage in the proceedings things begin to get noticeably unpleasant for Normal Malarkey.

Since the temper of a person deprived of crack is an awesome sight, but it has nothing on that of a person finding himself gazumped on it at the last minute. And now Normal Malarkey is faced with a posse of such persons, albeit briefly. Because suddenly his face is heading bootwards and floorwards and wallwards, yet all the time he is calling April, and even when being punted along the sitting-room carpet is still trying to peer under the sofa for any trace of her.

Whether the residents' hearts are touched by such devotion is open to question. For whatever reason, Normal Malarkey does not wake up in a box as might be expected but surrounded instead by ministering doctors & nurses & managers & accountants, having somehow found his way into intensive. Sadly he is unable to appreciate this good fortune, being in a state of triple pneumonia and advanced pain and general disorder, though while he rants and raves the name of April Ashby is never far from his lips. Indeed, the ministering doctors & managers are hearing so much about her that they feel like she is part of the family and are becoming heartily sick of her, while the bed-ridden patients all around Normal Malarkey are soon confounding medical opinion with the speed and urgency of their recoveries.

Pretty soon the only people who still wish to listen to Normal Malarkey are wearing unflattering shoes and asking him more questions than mastermind, because the forces of law & order are enthusiastic to learn why Normal Malarkey has been found face-down in a rubbish lorry and behaving as if he were part of the contents. But Normal Malarkey just waves his casts moodily in their direction and refuses to answer, since he is devoting all his hours & thoughts to April Ashby and is finding such legal chatter intrusive.

Now one morning Damage is being wheeled through the ward, having come off the A40 somewhat sooner than expected when he sees Normal Malarkey who by now everyone has forgotten existed. So Damage says,

'Normal,' in some astonishment, though the more he looks at him the less appropriate this byline seems to be.

Currently Normal Malarkey is muttering busily to himself, being intent on devising a route into the basement and back to April Ashby come hell or high water or, alternatively the instant he is liberated from traction. And when they realise that Damage not only knows Normal Malarkey but is seemingly still prepared to speak to him, the ministering nurses park his trolley by the bed and put the brake on before shooting off down the corridor heedless of Damage's plaintive cries, because Damage has never had much to say to Normal Malarkey even in passing.

But Normal Malarkey appears to be delighted to see Damage, since of course Damage is acquainted with April Ashby, and he is soon confiding his ideas with great enthusiasm. Damage is listening in some puzzlement, having no idea what he can be on about, until Normal Malarkey pauses for air and Damage says, 'But April Ashby is in Inverness. I just got a postcard,' and relapses into fond memories of April Ashby, and only after some time does he notice that Normal Malarkey is gazing at him in silence.

Eventually Normal Malarkey croaks, 'What?' so Damage continues saying oh yes, it appears she hooked up with a long-distance lorry driver somewhere outside Chearsley, you know April.

When all of a sudden the hospital air is rent with screams & cries of disbelief & rage, and Normal Malarkey is shouting, 'Tell me you are lying!' while trying to throttle Damage with his IV tubing. And Damage says in bewilderment all right all right I am lying. But Normal Malarkey does not believe him. Indeed he quietens down only when the ministering nurses give him his methadone dose, since thanks to weeks of hospital care Normal Malarkey becomes quite aggressive if he does not get his dose on time, if not sooner.

So when he finally limps out of hospital and back into town no one calls him normal any more. Even Guy & I do not have the heart to tackle him about the missing wizz, reckoning there is no point, because, on top of being on crutches and homeless and a meth addict and so on, Normal Malarkey now has not a penny to rub together.

For many weeks Normal Malarkey can be seen wandering the streets in this fashion, until eventually, like a homing pigeon, his path leads him down familiar roads and past familiar alleys and back to his old basement. On seeing him on the doorstep, the residents choke on their smoke in disbelief and comment, 'But you are dead in a lorry,' and Normal Malarkey looks most disconsolate and replies that he wishes he was, at which news the residents look more friendly. When they hear about Normal Malarkey's situation and the meth and so on they are feeling even more companionable, indeed in no time at all they are calling him Norm and apologising for the earlier misunderstanding. And in his turn Normal Malarkey finds it quite easy to forgive & forget, since the residents are soon urging him to join them in a rock or two, pointing out in a convivial manner that there is really no reason why not.

To which argument Normal Malarkey finds he has no sensible answers left, and presently the residents are watching him smoking like a pro, and smiling like proud parents, there being nothing people like better than seeing someone else adopt their bad habits, whether it is cigs or lager or rocks or whatever.

But fairly soon Normal Malarkey finds that his companions have grown tired of their generosity, and are withdrawing their supply, saying, 'You're a big boy, Norm. It is time you were paying for it.' This, of course, is only fair, though Normal Malarkey does not think so. Because shortly he can only think of rocks, and specifically of buying rocks, and then smoking rocks, and then buying more rocks and smoking those also, though possibly saving a few for later. But none of his companions seems inclined to advance him a penny to buy them regardless of the interest Normal Malarkey is promising, and neither does he have high hopes of a bank loan.

So left with no choice Normal Malarkey sails out into the street, where he is soon camouflaged behind a convenient pile of refuse and waiting for a rich person or similar to fall into his clutches. However, although time goes by nothing else obliges, and after a while Normal Malarkey's mind starts heading back to days of old and to another rubbish pile and to April Ashby, no matter how much he tries to divert it.

Because these memories are causing Normal Malarkey to feel most uncomfortable. In fact, at the thought of April Ashby seeing him in this condition he hangs his head in shame, and the more he considers matters the lower it hangs, until finally Normal Malarkey is crying like a baby among the cabbage leaves and assorted debris, because he is now nothing but an outcast & a junkie twice over, and no one of April Ashby's high standards will ever dream of loving him, or even asking him the time of day, and Normal Malarkey cannot blame her.

Eventually he sniffs to a stop feeling most sympathetic for himself and the position he is in and wishing more than ever that he could get himself out of it. When suddenly his eyes go blank, and although they are pointing in the direction of a baked bean tin they are seeing something else entirely, and moments later Normal Malarkey is shouting eureka behind the bin liners, and thanking heaven that he has not burnt his boats and embarked on a life of crime & robbery, for which he is not at all suited in the first place.

Because in his head Normal Malarkey is imagining a tattered yet curiously impressive figure arising from its hiding place behind the refuse and leaving the basement far behind. He pictures this figure marching towards the police station with its head held high, and when it gets there he sees it banging on the desk and saying, 'Take me to the chief constable, I have something to report,' in firm & public-spirited tones, after which there is a fade out. And the next thing Normal Malarkey sees is the figure being ushered into a large white interview room, where there follows a long session with many cups of coffee and free biscuits. And inside the room the figure is giving out names & dates & details of suppliers, and the atmosphere is tense and full of cig smoke and tape recorders, and blue-clad voices are muttering my god this is incredible. And although the tattered figure is obviously near fainting with exhaustion, it keeps itself upright with a will of iron and continues speaking in a concise & audible fashion. When it finally stops, the chief moves towards it saying, 'I would like to shake you by the hand, Norman Malarkey.'

Following this there are general cheers and the sound of a large cheque being written out to bearer, and the next day there are banner headlines in the Bucks Free Press saying UNDERCOVER OPERATIVE BREAKS DRUG RING, though actually Normal Malarkey thinks he will probably shun all publicity; in any case he will be spending the pay-off on a drug-free rest cure.

And once he is cured, which Normal Malarkey knows will be a painful though improving process, he will be able to visit April Ashby with pride in his heart and cash in his pocket, and although he is not betting she will leap into his arms at the sound of jingling, Normal Malarkey would not lay money against it either.

So he is wiping away tears of hope, and picturing April Ashby's face when he finds her, and is preparing to get up and visit the station and start his cure on the instant, when he hears the patter of footsteps along the path and looks out to see a housewifely shape advancing towards him. And the more Normal Malarkey looks, the more he sees that it is dangling a handbag from one arm in what he reckons to be a criminally negligent fashion.

As the handbag gets closer Normal Malarkey's eyes are glued to it in horror, because it is practically begging someone to snatch it. In fact, Normal Malarkey is only surprised that no one in the neighbourhood has jumped at the chance already. And here he thinks about calling out a warning, but for some reason he does not.

The handbag gets nearer and nearer, and it looks to be stuffed full of good things, and then all of a sudden it pauses in front of Normal Malarkey's nose, and waves at him in a most enticing manner, since the housewifely shape is turning round & round in an attempt to get its bearings. But Normal Malarkey's gaze is still stapled on the handbag and the next thing, Normal Malarkey leaps out of his refuse and is trying to hug the handbag to his breast, since he is thinking that his cure will be much easier and more pleasant if he can just get a little smoke in first.

But the housewifely shape seems reluctant to contribute to such a good cause; instead it is clutching the handbag with conviction and giving Normal Malarkey a few kicks in addition, and Normal Malarkey is hurt and wounded by this conservative approach and is giving a few kicks back again. Eventually the figure subsides to the pavement, but not after putting Normal Malarkey to a great deal of trouble on its behalf, so he adds a few more kicks and so on for good measure.

After which Normal Malarkey returns to the basement glowing with triumph & physical exertion, and is attacking the handbag zip when he hears a feeble banging on the front door accompanied by a rattling

of the handle. But by now Normal Malarkey has visions
of rocks the size of Everest dancing in front of his eyes,
which naturally he finds somewhat distracting, so he
turns a blind ear and begins rummaging through the
handbag with great anticipation.

He is emptying the contents on the floor when down
the hallway comes a faint female voice giving out a distress call. And the voice is calling help, help and also
Norman, Norman, but by this time Normal Malarkey is
gazing at his spoils and finding they consist of an old
keyring and the total sum of £3.56, which will not get
him so much as a pebble at current market prices. And
Normal Malarkey's face is falling, and he barely hears
the voice through his annoyance and disappointment,
and so he hardly notices when, after a while, the voice
dies away altogether.

E L E V E N

Of course there are many mad people in Aylesbury, and it is a source of great comfort to the authorities that they all inhabit the market square benches, it being impossible otherwise to succour them, or move them on when they annoy the rest of population or every fifteen minutes, whichever happens sooner. And this policy is called care in the community, and is widely held to be a winner and a budget saver, though once in a while someone fails to realise the advantages of the scheme and goes mad inside a council house or similar, often with distasteful consequences, which leaves the authorities going tsk tsk tsk at such inconsiderate behaviour.

But generally everyone knows what goes where. And so reporting for bench duty every morning are characters such as oven-ready Brian, who always wears tin-foil to pick up alien transmissions; and Wiggy, who wears eight wigs at once; and Mad Ethel, who does not wear anything of interest but qualifies on account of her christian name. Along with an assortment of people going mumble mumble aardvark mumble; not to mention the old alkies, who claim that they are not mad at all, theirs being quite a sensible option in modern society, with the result that they are relegated to a bench of their own and are popularly considered inferior.

Now one Saturday the customary peace & order of this little community is much disturbed. Indeed the mumbling and muttering is sounding like a beehive, and though the old alkies are still crying spare us 50p for a croissant at passing shoppers in an attempt to maintain routine, for once no other voices are joining them. Because sitting in the middle of Mad Ethel's bench, in fact just where Mad Ethel is accustomed to sitting, is a small, black, wrinkled character, with a smile of great beauty on his face and a cig dangling from his lips, and standing behind him is a large, white, cowlike person wearing a vacant & devoted expression. And oven-ready Brian is prodding the former in some excitement and shouting, 'An alien!' there being not that many black faces in Aylesbury though a great many purple ones.

But otherwise the reception is not a welcoming one, the bench population being somewhat possessive about their seats as indeed shoppers & mothers & exhausted old grannies frequently discover. So after a time the black character is heard to say, 'Come,' to his sidekick, in what sounds like an american accent, after which they repair with some dignity to a deserted bench at a distance.

And as the black character repairs he takes with him a man-sized white wooden cross, which he is wearing with some difficulty in an over-the-shoulder look. This outfit casts even oven-ready Brian's in the shade, and many of the benchers appear more than a little impressed by this novel get-up, though others are muttering who does he think he is? in an aggrieved fashion. But the Cross Man, as he naturally comes to be known, says nothing.

It is only when the forces of law & order arrive in their punctual way and begin saying move along now, move along that everyone realises what they are dealing with.

Since the bench population and the forces of law & order have long ago given up taking this routine personally, it not being worth the bother on either side. And though the constables wave their truncheons in a threatening manner and the benchers spit scornfully on the floor and say police brutality and so on, it is really all very civilised with honours generally equal.

*   *   *

But either the Cross Man has not read this script or he does not feel it extends him sufficiently, because when the constables approach his bench wearing eager faces at the sight of a fresh & ethnic challenge, the Cross Man leaps on top of his bench and brandishes his cross and roars, 'Jesus is love,' in a voice like a lion, which is remarkable coming from a person resembling an old black grape, and which has the constables grinding to a halt and looking at each other in some anxiety.

'Do you,' the Cross Man continues from above them at three-thousand decibels, 'do you love Jesus?' and he gazes down at the constables with an expression of extreme doubt, and though one constable is heard to reply yes, he doubtless regrets it in the police canteen after.

'Ladies & gentlemen,' bellows the Cross Man, since by now quite a crowd is collecting around him. 'These men,' and here he pauses with a face of sorrow, 'these men are not churchgoers.' After which there are many boos and hisses from the floor, and especially from those who would not be dragged near a church by wild horses unless it had lead roofing. Guy, who is among them, sees that the Cross Man sensibly does not push his luck, since he steps off the bench and dons his cross, and moves meekly off with his sidekick in the direction of the other benchers, leaving his audience baying for more, though not the constables.

Now currently it is summertime & the living is easy & the general population are washing their lawns and hoovering their cars as prescribed, and finding that this still leaves ten hours to fill even if they add in weeding. So the sudden appearance of the Cross Man raises much interest and discussion, and come next Saturday there are many shoppers loitering in the market square. But there is no sign of a resurrection, so the square has a disgruntled air about it and people are preparing to pass by, when a little procession emerges from underneath the arches and cuts off their exit.

At the front is the Cross Man smiling most beatifically, and after him comes a trail of old alkies smirking self-consciously, and the procession winds round to the middle of the market square, where the Cross Man steps on to a bench and thunders, 'Praise the lord these wonderful people are saved.' And the old alkies are chorusing saved, saved, and watching the Cross Man like lynxes because he is brandishing a bottle of sainsbury's rum in the air, which he proceeds to pour on to the cobbles, booming, 'Poison,' in a sorrowful manner.

The old alkies watch it trickle into the gutter in a pre-occupied fashion, but at the applause that follows this demo they take heart and begin a ragged chorus of jesus wants me for a sunbeam, and before the crowd know it they are digging deep into their pockets and shelling cash into the old alkies' outstretched paws. Since seemingly people are prepared to shell out without qualms in this manner, even though getting a penny off them beforehand is like a pound of flesh. And the next Saturday the old alkies' bench is reverberating to lord of the dance and other popular tunes and if the alkies are hiccuping somewhat in between choruses everyone is putting it down to natural emotion & gratitude.

Thus from this flying start the Cross Man is up and running, and every Saturday he preaches in a loud & saintly manner from the middle of the market square, surrounded by alkies and also pigeons doing their best to look like doves and not quite getting there, since the Aylesbury pigeon in its natural state mostly resembles an old dishcloth.

At first the other bench inhabitants put their noses in the air and remain aloof, considering this type of public spectacle most distasteful, but gradually they look more & more as if they are wallflowers at a party, and one by one they begin uprooting themselves and sidling into the centre. And shortly even the bench people who say mumble mumble are wearing little white crosses where their lapels used to be and trying to sing jesus loves me this I know though it is rarely they get beyond the first letter. Which leaves only Mad Ethel and Wiggy sitting haughtily in solitary, as after a few weeks even oven-ready Brian is won over by the talk of heavenly bodies and so on and decamps.

By now the Cross Man is becoming something of a tourist attraction or at any rate more of one than the civic, and is getting more donations than oxfam, because like it or not shoppers are forced to pass through the market square, all roads leading to it like Rome. And the Cross Man refreshes these weary consumers with many a reviving hymn, while more practically his disciple hands out fish paste sarnies and orange squash, and also little white crosses all free of charge & gratis, which he picks up off the cobbles at the end of each session in a green & recycling manner.

On top of these day trippers, Aylesbury turns out to contain several hundred-per-cent christians, and shortly they have adopted the Cross Man as something of a mascot; indeed they can be seen carolling alongside him and applauding themselves in the manner of quiz-show contestants.

But despite this popularity on the ground it seems that the Cross Man is causing much envy in high places, with charities and church leaders and the forces of law & order presently grinding their teeth whenever they see a crucifix. Because the population are feeling they have done their bit in the market square every Saturday, and they show no sign of wishing to repeat this spiritual experience, especially as, unlike the Cross Man, the charities and churches are comparatively lacking in the entertainment & snack factor. The result is that church attendances are apparently threatening to drop out of double figures, and charity boxes are being brought back empty apart from a button, even without being tampered with first. And the forces of law & order are having to explain that, although they are practised & professional at breaking up most things e.g. rallies, raves, parties, front doors etc, they are less accustomed to breaking up a christian sing-song, and indeed feel that any attempt to do so will leave them looking somewhat foolish.

Now the community are more or less ignoring this situation, other than to revel a little in the authorities' discomfort, and Guy & I also find the messages of peace & love and so on pass us by. Guy is currently preoccupied with a new & blooming organisation known as the Town Centre Element, who call themselves the TCE for short and ease of spelling. When the TCE first appear, the Aylesbury Skins naturally think they are a hoot, owing to the fact that they all wear baggy trousers and rings and built-up trainers and it is also rumoured hair gel. But the TCE soon prove that they have more than a casual acquaintance with multi gyms and steroids by declaring war on the Aylesbury Skins, though most unfairly they do not bother informing the skins of the outbreak of hostilities. Instead they are lying in wait round corners & picking off the smaller skins one by one, so that by the time the skins realise what is occurring it is too late to do any physical preparation and they are having to fall back on raw cunning and bike chains. However, it seems that these tactics are paying off, and Guy is organising many successful raids into TCE territory and swaggering round like Napoleon, and saying pleasure before business whenever I point out that I am doing all the work in the meantime.

One morning we are snatching a quick cup of tea in Anna's caff along with ex-uncle Nigel, who is down from Manchester for the day on some business or other, though when asked he replies none of yours. And ex-uncle Nigel is extolling the joys of the north, and indeed is looking like a new person, or at least one that has had a make-over, when all of a sudden he pauses mid-mouthful and after some spluttering enquires, 'Who is that?' while pointing out of the window with an agitated finger.

Guy & I see that it is only the Cross Man, who for once is without a disciple in sight and appears to be window shopping in Burtons. So we give ex-uncle Nigel a brief résumé, and ex-uncle Nigel looks most thoughtful and returns his eyes for a second scan. After which ex-uncle Nigel says that if that is an American bible-basher he is dutch, in fact unless he is much mistaken it is none other than a scottish gent known as

Lefty MacGuire, who he has not seen since his Scrubs days. The reason he is fairly convinced is that while inside Lefty MacGuire has his earlobe chewed off by a cellmate, and when examined the Cross Man is also missing an earlobe, though on reflection ex-uncle Nigel cannot be sure it is the right one.

But then ex-uncle Nigel enquires if the Cross Man is ever seen around or near a kid. Guy & I think about this and realise that he never is, since his sidekick is always whipping away any kid before they get within spitting distance, and silencing any cries of disagreement with a lolly. So ex-uncle Nigel slaps his thigh and says that that proves it, Lefty MacGuire having always hated children with a vengeance; in fact they turn out to be his undoing.

It seems that back in those days Lefty MacGuire is a notorious conman and jackanory artist, though the reason he is notorious is not because anyone ever believes him. On the contrary, while other conmen of the period are having a high time impersonating bank managers & solicitors & aristocrats and so on, Lefty MacGuire is left with only a limited range of options and ekes out a living by doing Paul Robeson or Daley Thompson and occasionally the Nigerian ambassador. And although these disguises are getting Lefty MacGuire into nightclubs and sporting occasions, and once in a while off a speeding ticket, every time he tries to persuade the public to sink capital into one of his copper-bottomed schemes they look at him askance and say, 'Oh, yes, bananas is it?' in mocking voices, and refuse to sink a penny. Which narrow-minded approach ex-uncle Nigel personally finds most reprehensible, and he says it is not surprising that Lefty MacGuire should become somewhat embittered. Because to supplement his income he soon resorts to a conman's old stand-by in times of hardship, which is being a magician at kiddies' parties. But unfortunately Lefty MacGuire is operating in Glasgow at the time, where it seems that kiddies are not kiddies at all but piranhas, and Lefty MacGuire's main challenge is getting to the household valuables & cash before his audience snaps them up first.

On top of which Lefty MacGuire is not much of a magician, and the Glasgow infants do not take kindly to the sight of Lefty MacGuire stammering & sweating & magically producing handkerchiefs from his pockets. In fact, Lefty MacGuire is generally exiting from these sessions by the skin of his teeth and sometimes via a window, and after a while he starts to introduce himself on such occasions as Herod.

But despite his lack of patter and tricks, Lefty MacGuire has a pièce de résistance. All his life he is into racing pigeons, and for many years the pride & joy of his flock is a bird named Ruby, who he hand-raises from an egg.

Ruby is by all accounts a pearl among pigeons, being sleek & glossy & streamlined like a greyhound, and in addition to these assets she possesses a loving nature and is always cooing into Lefty MacGuire's ear and giving his cheek affectionate pecks and so on. With the result that Lefty MacGuire is forever maintaining he would not swap Ruby for any human bird, since in his experience women never act that way even when they want something.

And unlike Lefty MacGuire Ruby takes to magic like a duck to water, and is hopping professionally out of his jacket on command and seemingly enjoying all the attention, though Lefty MacGuire is reluctant to exploit her talents and will produce her only on special occasions.

Now one afternoon it seems to be getting that way, since Lefty MacGuire is decorated in shades of jelly & trifle and finds himself backed into a corner by an infant mob baying for blood, but the last thing he wants is to expose Ruby to any of this unpleasantness. So it is with horror that he hears the infants beginning a chant of out out out, because inside his jacket Ruby is recognising her call to action, and despite Lefty MacGuire's best efforts, Ruby emerges from his breast and flutters sedately about the room, after which she looks round for the top hat on which she is accustomed to taking her bow.

ANIMALS ❑

Apparently Lefty MacGuire will never discuss what
happens next, saying that there are sights a man prefers
to forget even if they return to haunt his dreams ever
after. But anyway it is something to do with a three-bar
electric fire, and while Lefty MacGuire is weeping tears
of horror and attempting to throttle the child who
wielded the baseball bat, the child's mother enters and
on seeing her son & heir limp and purple, naturally
calls for assistance.

Lefty MacGuire is led off in chains and spends a most
trying time inside, because no matter how much he
tries to explain events, the word gets round that he is
an infant abuser. And what happens to infant abusers in
the comfort of their cells is the stuff of legend, though
Lefty MacGuire discovers it to be reasonably accurate,
even once he is transferred down to the Scrubs for his
own safety. So by the time Lefty MacGuire exits he is
foaming at the mouth whenever a kid is so much as
mentioned, having had no need of the aversion therapy
he has been given in the first place.

But that, says ex-uncle Nigel, is many years ago, and
he is pleased to see that Lefty MacGuire is back on
form and earning a decent living, since the last thing
he hears Lefty MacGuire has hooked up with a very
unpleasant type in the protection business, who is
known as Mr Frederick Jones, on account of no one
daring to call him anything else. Though, ex-uncle

Nigel adds, you would not credit it to look at him, as Mr Frederick Jones resembles nothing more unpleasant than a friendly heifer, which it seems is partly the secret of his success, the other part being nail-guns.

On hearing that Lefty MacGuire does indeed have such a character in tow, ex-uncle Nigel turns rather pale and remembers a train he is missing, and hastily departs saying yes well there will always be a welcome in Manchester, after which Guy and I move to the Bell and soon dismiss all thoughts of this craven approach with many refreshing bevvies.

But presently we are wishing that we had paid more attention to ex-uncle Nigel because Mr Frederick Jones is seen to be deep in conversation with Guy's opposite number on the TCE, who is as large as Guy but twice as ugly, or so Guy maintains. And no one can think what the TCE's chief & leader and Mr Frederick Jones might have to talk about, but they are laying twenty to one it is not the weather.

And the following Saturday, Lefty MacGuire makes his entrance into the market square bang on schedule, but this time instead of old alkies he is followed by the full TCE contingent all of whom are sporting little white cross badges on their silk T-shirts. When this entourage reaches the centre, Lefty MacGuire clears his throat rather nervously and announces praise the lord these wonderful people are saved etc, and there are many sceptical looks and cries of saved my backside from around the square. But Lefty MacGuire holds up a reproachful hand and points out that even the most miserable sinner can be saved, it is in the bible. And when everyone comes to think about it it is, although the TCE are not looking any too happy at being described as miserable sinners and are casting dark glances in Lefty MacGuire's direction.

Nevertheless, for the next couple of weeks Aylesbury is reeling in shock as the crime rate shoots downwards, and soon old grannies are roaming the streets free of fear, and girls are wearing short skirts without considering the consequences, and shopkeepers are barely bothering with their shutters & alarms & electrified grilles and so on. Because on top of being saved themselves, it seems that the TCE are intent on persuading everyone else to act likewise, and most of Aylesbury's smaller villains find the TCE's powers of persuasion irresistible and hastily move their attentions to Wycombe.

Of course, no one is too bothered by what happens in Wycombe, and although the Aylesbury police are moaning and complaining like anything about this new development the population are generally agreeing that it is only jealousy, because the police are always

encouraging neighbourhood watch schemes and similar, which are exactly the same only useless.

So when Mr Frederick Jones starts visiting shops &
pubs & bars and other sites of interest rattling a collection box with join the fight for jesus written on the side,
most of the owners are only too happy to cough up even
if they are lifelong atheists. Because Mr Frederick Jones
assures them that jesus will doubtless pay them special
attention if they do not, though otherwise he will save
them a small fortune on their insurance premiums.

And one morning Anna wakes to find smoke and all
her pasties and sausages cooking without the benefit
of a frying pan, and stepping out into the street she
discovers that the caff is burning like a toasted sarnie,
having informed Mr Frederick Jones where to put his
collection box, and not politely.

Naturally the business storeroom goes up in flames
along with the pasties, and when the fire brigade finish
among the fumes they are looking unnaturally cheerful
and some are giggling. But Guy & I are not, since the
contents are not insured. So we are sitting in the civic
coming to terms with this, and attempting to ignore
Damage, who these days is almost impossible to ignore,
being on a wizz kick more than usual, and indeed is
behaving in a most irritating manner, and prodding Guy
and me every time we do not applaud his monologues.

Currently Damage is enthusing about the latest game he has discovered, which is chicken. And the world according to Damage is divided into two types of people, although this excludes the many drivers who, on suddenly finding themselves playing chicken with him, will cry what the hell and take instant evasive action in a hedgerow, because these people Damage dismisses out of hand as of no account & irrelevant.

The first type of person, Damage explains, is the sort who look like they are keeping their nerve until the very last minute, at which point they will say fuck it and bottle out. And in this category Damage places just about everyone. But the other type, Damage says somewhat boastfully, is the type who will say fuck it in a carefree manner and keep their foot down no matter what, and naturally Damage puts himself in this bracket, and is saying that it is only a shame there are not more like him on the road, as he is getting most frustrated.

Throughout this discourse Guy & I are going mmm, but eventually Guy's patience snaps its tether, which is never a long one. Damage exits muttering, and Guy returns to swearing vengeance on Mr Frederick Jones and Lefty MacGuire, since he is taking the attack on Anna's caff personally, in fact more personally than Anna, who despite her fury is consoling herself with thoughts of insurance and possibly a burger bar in

Blackpool. But no matter how much Guy plots & schemes he can see no light ahead of him, because by now Mr Frederick Jones and Lefty MacGuire are local heroes, on top of which they are protected by the TCE in the manner of a bank vault.

Guy is reluctantly admitting that he does not think the skins are up to cracking it, when a dark shadow looms over the table and he leaps to his feet like a gunfighter, because the shadow belongs to the hulking form of the TCE chief & leader. Guy is obviously resenting this intrusion and preparing to draw when the TCE chief & leader says no, I come in peace, very hastily, so Guy removes his hand from his pocket and, casting a scornful look at Eddie the manager who is wailing not here for gawd's sake, sits down again, though slowly.

Now the TCE chief & leader, who goes by the name of Vernon, is wearing an expression of inner turmoil. And over a few bevvies it transpires that he is as keen to get shot of Mr Frederick Jones as Guy, if not more so. Because ever since Mr Frederick Jones comes on the scene Vernon finds his status dwindling and his authority wilting; indeed by now it is Mr Frederick Jones who is TCE chief & leader in all but name, since the TCE are so dazzled by the riches & power & fame he is offering them, it is all Vernon can do to remind them who is elected in the first place.

*   *   *

But, despite this common ground, time passes without a solution, since Vernon is soon admitting that, much as he would like to call the TCE off, he fears they will no longer be receptive. Eventually he announces that he will have to make tracks, being down to look after his kid sister; though personally, he says he would rather face a squad of skins armed only with a toothpick, his sister being like that. And at this news Guy & I gaze at Vernon with some interest and say oh really.

The next Saturday is ascension or pentecost or easter monday, or at any rate an event of major interest in the religious calendar. So the market square is full of clapping christians on top of the usual contraflow of bench people and shoppers, and when Lefty MacGuire appears the shouts of praise the lord rattle the windows and Lefty MacGuire mounts his portable pulpit with a face of peace & love & satisfaction at the turn-out, though this is soon dropping into his sandals.

Because making his way through the crowd is Guy, and in one hand he is brandishing a little cross so all the christians are murmuring praise be etc as he passes. And in the other he is brandishing a kid, and though the kid is noticeably grubby and worn around the edges and is trying to get its teeth into Guy's kneecaps, all the housewives & mothers are going ah at the sight of an infant in a pavlovian manner.

*　　*　　*

Lefty MacGuire eyes this vision with obvious revulsion, and then casts his eyes round for Mr Frederick Jones or the TCE to save him. But at the moment many skins are using Mr Frederick Jones as a sofa, though judging by his muffled curses it would appear that he is not relishing this experience; indeed, it is taking the skins much skill and balance to stay on him. And in another corner Vernon is distracting the TCE by announcing plans for expansion Wycombe way, so the TCE are in a huddle discussing who should head up this new venture, and from the many sounds of disagreement it seems that all of them wish to apply. So Lefty MacGuire is left facing Guy and the kid, and Guy looks him straight in the eye and says, 'Bless this child.'

Lefty MacGuire starts sweating and shivering like a horse scenting blood and passes his hand over his brow many times, and the crowd senses something is up and falls silent. And Guy repeats his request, and releases the kid from his iron grip, at which the kid belts forward, and Guy & I wait in anticipation, since Vernon guarantees his kid sister will go for Lefty MacGuire like a pitbull.

But instead the kid stops in front of Lefty MacGuire's wrinkled old features and says, 'Brown,' in some astonishment, because no one has thought to brief it that Lefty MacGuire is a black person. After which the kid smiles and says it likes brown people and blows Lefty MacGuire a little kiss.

And Lefty MacGuire looks sick, but manages a bless you in a revolted voice, and the kid skips off. So it seems that all the planning & plotting is for nothing; indeed it is turning to ashes, on top of which Mr Frederick Jones is now calling out help help to the TCE and, despite Vernon's best efforts, it is only a matter of time before they start to pay attention.

When all at once the air is rent by the sound of rich and strange oaths, and Lefty MacGuire is leaping down from the pulpit and roaring, 'Och ye fuckin wee bastid are ye gaunny leave that alaine or am I away after deckin ye?' and so on.

Since on the way back the kid has spotted an Aylesbury pigeon which is slouching around the cobbles in a sullen fashion, or is until the kid aims a kick at it in passing. And the pigeon rises two inches and then settles again, so the kid gives it a rerun, until eventually there comes the satisfying noise of pigeon connecting with a trainer.

And Lefty MacGuire is now clutching the kid and agitating it like a magimix and bellowing be nice to animals, and although this message is a christian one the language which accompanies it is not. The kid is howling & bellowing back and chomping any bits of Lefty MacGuire within reach, so it is looking quite an even contest until both parties disappear under a pile of assorted mothers and christians and shop assistants.

The mothers are shouting unhand that child you monster and the christians are shouting fake and phoney and the shop assistants are shouting with delight at the opportunity to liven up their lunchbreak, so the TCE finally agree to postpone their discussion, being reluctant to miss the fun & exercise.

Then Vernon shouts, 'Look at Frederick Jones,' because somewhere along the line Mr Frederick Jones has got clear of the skins, and instead of galloping to his partner's rescue he is tiptoeing very quietly round a corner.

On seeing their idol displaying these feet of clay the TCE are naturally disappointed. Indeed they are soon encouraging Mr Frederick Jones to reconsider, but he remains adamant, and when the TCE attempt to pull him back he becomes quite aggressive, which is unfortunate, because of course Mr Frederick Jones is one and the TCE are many.

After watching this activity for a while Guy & I adjourn to the civic, where we are soon enjoying a quiet bevvy and listening with some satisfaction to the wail of

sirens and screech of police vans outside, when a
small and bedraggled figure hurtles past the windows
with a mob of christians in hot pursuit. And the figure
is clutching a stunned & thoughtful pigeon to its breast,
so we see it is Lefty MacGuire.

Lefty MacGuire is getting off to a bad start, being
somewhat hampered in this fashion, and the christians
are scenting victory and clutching at his coat-tails, and
for a second it looks as though he is going under. But
suddenly the pigeon stirs and opens an eye and starts
to revive and flap in an encouraging fashion, and at this
sight Lefty MacGuire seems to take heart and puts on a
burst of speed. And by the time he rounds the corner
the christians are dropping back into second, until
eventually they give up all hope and stand panting &
fulminating, as by now Lefty MacGuire and the pigeon
are making for the open highway and running as if on
wings.

T W E L V E

Now first thing Monday, Anna, our one-time friend and supplier, departs for good & for Blackpool, and the same morning Guy & I reckon up our resources and discover that we are left with only a small brick of hash and sundry wraps and pills, which is not promising. And by lunchtime we agree that it looks as though the business is heading the way of all flesh and most businesses and is about to disintegrate altogether, and when we recover from this sobering thought, which is over an afternoon bevvy or several in the Kings Head, we decide to take the brick to Manchester and see if we cannot build it up into something bigger & better for our retirement. So, by the time the stars surface, ex-uncle Nigel is ready & waiting and the capri boot is packed and we are performing a farewell lap of honour round the market square, though this is owing less to sentiment and more to the one-way system.

The Kings Head doors are wide open and many of

the community are there shouting encouragement and throwing affectionate cans and so on, and Guy & I look at all the old familiar faces and notice with some relief that Damage is not among them, it being generally agreed that Damage's reaction on finding that the remaining wizz stock is heading north would be more than a little hasty. Though under some pressure Bernie has offered to break the news gently to him later, as long as it is in public and a well-lit environment.

And the capri is overflowing with notes and scribbled IOUs because the community are counting on us to send back supplies & brighten their darker hours, and also with much rejoicing and cheer, because Guy & I are finding the idea of broadening our horizons not unpleasant. And shortly we are broaching wraps & cans in honour of the occasion, and the capri is doing a ton on similar grounds, and we are turning up the sound and agreeing that it seems like Aylesbury is already far behind us, though in fact it is not.

Since all of a sudden we notice many shops and cars and overflowing bins and consequently realise that we are still on the High St. So Guy is slowing down in a law-abiding manner, feeling it preferable not to get stopped under the circs, when we see distant lights in the mirror, and Guy slows down even more, which proves to be a mistake.

Because out of nowhere appears what looks to be a

porsche 944, and on catching up with the capri it does not indicate or signal or manoeuvre, but rams us playfully instead, and Guy & I & the capri lurch forward at which point the porsche waggles its pop-up headlights and does it again.

After a short while the porsche obviously feels this is lacking something in entertainment, because it then pulls up alongside us, and the window slides down and Damage's face appears in the gap. He is laughing and waving and pointing to the back of the capri and inviting us to share the joke, but Guy & I do not; indeed we are having problems seeing it at all.

Since the porsche continues to nudge our side in a friendly manner, and Guy is having to fight to stay on the road, which Damage apparently finds most amusing as he is pulling back and letting us get ahead and then coming back for a rerun, and all the time he is laughing his head off, though sadly not literally. And although Guy is speaking sternly to the capri and attempting to pull away, the capri is now struggling & groaning and not finding the legs despite its game attempts. But suddenly Damage gives a mock salute and the porsche disappears off the road, and from behind us we hear the triumphant sound of sirens.

So Guy rolls his eyes and I suggest that this will be the shortest car chase in living memory, as our wheels are wobbling and the capri is now proceeding down the High St at a geriatric pace, and Guy is stopping for traffic lights in a sarcastic way and suggesting that perhaps we should pull over & wait for them. But of course we do not, and instead we continue to potter along in this fashion, there being no convenient turn-off in sight, and meanwhile I lean out of the window and keep out an eye or two for the pursuit. And I am soon regretfully informing Guy that the forces of law & order have rounded the market square and are heading down the High St like maniacs; indeed, it is a wonder no one has been hurt already.

Guy is saying it is typical and so on, and I am enjoying the night air and admiring the passing window displays, when from behind us comes the sudden cry of a pedestrian surprised on a zebra. On looking back I see the pedestrian is currently underneath a panda, and many police officers are standing beside it and scratching their heads and otherwise looking somewhat embarrassed.

And though after an interval the sirens start up again in the distance, they are sounding noticeably more apologetic than before, and indeed they soon fade away altogether.

For a time the capri limps along without a word, as neither of us are yet ready to mention Damage, and it is only when we are coming into Chearsley and heading past the bus shelter that we break this thoughtful silence. Indeed Guy breaks it by shouting fucker after which he opines that whether Damage has found out about the trip or is just doing what comes naturally, this time he goes too far, and if it were not for Manchester he, Guy, would shortly be visiting Damage with a sledgehammer on account of what he has done to the capri, which is Guy's pride & joy though, by the sounds of it, not for much longer. And I am inclined to agree with him.

But soon I turn up the sound and start rolling like a production line, and Guy is passing over cans and we are speculating as to the nature of Manchester, which ex-uncle Nigel is always saying is a world of opportunity & pleasure, though we do not credit ex-uncle Nigel for a second and agree that it is probably along the same lines as London, and anyway will doubtless be a breeze. And these thoughts are carrying us gently over the brow of the hill, where we see the whole of the valley below us and the lights of Long Crendon twinkling on the hill opposite, and Guy winds down his window and takes a deep breath and then says through gritted teeth, 'Damage.'

Since the valley in front of us is deserted and the road behind us silent, but on top of the next hill are a pair of car headlights facing our direction, and they are in the centre of the road and not moving any closer. And as we watch in some fascination we see the lights dip & rise in greeting, after which they begin moving down the hill and straight towards us.

So Guy & I look at each other and say that does it, and Guy jams his foot down to the carpet and I am helpfully saying right a bit etc to get the capri centred, and the capri is making a last ditch effort & shooting forward.

With the hill and the following breeze and so on it is fast cracking along as if in its former glory, and soon we are close enough to hear Damage's music booming across the night air, and I am turning the capri sound up in retaliation, and shortly we are hearing the porsche exhaust over both of them. And Damage is keeping straight at us, and the capri is not faltering, and Guy & I are whooping & yelling in unison, as we are clutching cans and the music is loud and things are looking more than usually interesting. And right at the last minute Guy says, 'Fuck it,' and glances across for confirmation & I am inclined to agree with him.